THE PLAN

IMOGENE NIX

Thanks to everyone for giving me the opportunity to share this great little story.
I hope you fall a little in love with Jonah, just like I did all those years ago, when I first thought Oh My God!
Now it's back in my hands and reworked. The essence of the story remains the same though.
So enjoy the ride!
Imogene

Newsletter

Click on the image and sign up to my newsletter to receive a free book delivered to your inbox!

Chapter One

The girl they needed to find had gotten away and the frustration inside him welled at the knowledge of that one fact. Captain Jonah Fielding had caught a quick view of the little sprite running away. But even with a glance, he had the impression of a woman with a short and slight build, her red hair bobbing as she sprinted back toward the ship.

He'd spied her tripping over and falling down the steps that led to the ground outside the pros-house, which would have taken most freighter captains down for good. He watched in amazement as she rose and kept going, albeit a lot slower than before the fall. She seemed confident of her direction though. The girl eventually sidled into an authorized pros-tablishment near the port, his men missing the back door until it was too late. She had eluded his team.

He sighed again, the sound of his frustration echoing. His men did the best job they knew how to do, but were mainly untrained; all but a few he would categorize as unfit and unhealthy. The number of new recruits had been necessary on Centauri after the dismissal of a great many officers. The months of hard work stemmed his investigation into the rampant corruption and had stretched his resources thin, so he took what men he could get. For now anyway, he reminded himself.

Something about this case smelled like a week old dishrag though. He needed to find the girl fast, as well as the answer to why. Why she was prepared to handle the BXM parts when no one else in their right mind would? His sneaking suspicion was paired together with a fair heaping of thrown to the wolves—a sacrifice to get him off the tail of others, whose loss would have more of an impact on the illegal trade he guessed.

Sure, she may be running BXM parts, but the particular ones she carried weren't strictly considered high priority. The thoughts tumbled in his head as he mulled over the situation.

"Cap'n, she got away." The youngest member of his crew lifted gray eyes sadly. At nineteen, he had a long way to go, but he trained hard and was committed. What's more, he had a brain, morals, and a conscience; all three would stand him in good stead one day. For now though, he learned as he served with the Authority Department.

"McIntyre, I am aware of this. But can you tell me why?" Jonah needed to be patient with this youngster, train him well, so he had a good future with the Authority. In this one young man, Jonah saw the future of the department. That thought alone gave him heart to continue in the currently joyless task that he called his daily life.

"Cap'n? 'Cause she's a fast runner?" McIntyre's earnest voice filled the silence and Jonah bit back a groan.

The kid's father and uncle were both dead, killed in the purges of the corrupt Authorities who had controlled Centauri and the Space Ports. Jonah felt responsible for the growth of this youngster as a professional Authority staff member, if for no other reason, except he was one of his team. After that came the swirl of owing it to the dead. He cut the thought off and refocused.

"Partially, yes. Many of you are not fit, but apart from this, she has knowledge of the alleys and corridors of the space-port here. That means she is well known here and we may be able to wiggle some information from possible informants."

McIntyre's eyes shone with the information shared, and Jonah followed McIntyre's gaze, noting how his eyes glazed while passing it over in his mind, considering what he had been told. He would do well with good training. Jonah smiled.

* * *

Kadie's back ached, as did her legs, head, and even fingers. The lights of the console lit up in front of her, shining dimly in the gloom. *How could I be so stupid?* The words chased around in her brain as she throttled the ship back, searching for the right place to land. Finding a safe hiding space in this part of the galaxy was difficult unless you knew your way around like the back of your hand. Not that Kadie could lay claim to that, but she knew this section well enough.

She guided the small ship into the entry of a dark cavern hidden in the wilderness of a small asteroid belt. The ship hovered over the surface for a moment, and then she allowed the craft to drop slowly to the floor. A hiss rattled through the ship as it touched down, and she closed her eyes. She sighed, breathing in deeply and expanding her chest fully before exhaling.

Kadie rose from her seat, casting her gaze around the small, cluttered bridge. "I should never have agreed to help them." She muttered the words from between clenched teeth as she moved awkwardly toward the doorway, both knees screaming in pain from the fall she had taken earlier.

Combined with the hours of sitting in the chair, she had stinging knees and excruciating stiffness.

As she left the bridge, Kadie authorized the safety shields on her craft to engage and told the ship to enter lock-down. Thunks and clunks filled the air, but she couldn't even summon up the energy to grimace at the sounds.

Moving slowly through the ship was a nightmare as she limped along, relying on the walls for support. Kadie hadn't had time to assess her injuries when she left Centauri; the rush to take off and ensure her path couldn't be followed while in space had taken her total concentration. Besides, she wasn't prepared to rely on her old ship's automatic piloting program. It was so erratic that one time she had logged in a course and it had taken her hours to backtrack to the point of origin before heading to the actual rendezvous point. Needless to say, there had been a missed opportunity.

So here she was, hours on, still experiencing the churning, cold sensation as she remembered her evasion of the Authority man and his team. Yet, even as she tried to avoid remembering it, something niggled at the back of her mind.

I need to visit the sick bay, Kadie told herself as her head ached. She entered the spartan room, not seeing the cool, white walls or floor as she lowered herself down to the medibed, dropping the coveralls to her waist. The whole time, her fingers stung from her fumbled movements.

"Engage the medical droid." Her voice strained and sounded tired as she gave the command.

Lights blinked on in the alcove as she watched. This was one purchase she remained thankful for over and over again, even though it had cost her thousands of hard earned credits...credits she didn't have. Any freighter pilot understood basic med staff cost more, so she had scraped what she could together, begging and bartering enough to be able to afford the investment.

She laid back, the bare skin of her back prickling from the feel of the cool bed surface, watching as the shiny droid emerged from the safety shaft that had been retrofitted for its storage.

"Good evening, Miss Kadie. Let me see your injuries please." The cold, metal hands made a slow pass with the medi-scanner over her. "You have some deep contusions."

Kadie grimaced at the careful tone that she had activated when she first purchased the medi-droid. Yet, between the choices of the five default voice types, this was the one she found least offensive.

"Yes, I know that. Patch me up so I can go to bed." She cut the metallic voice off partway through the sentence. She didn't want a diplomatic, doctor-like interaction, and the voice override meant she could cut it off mid-stream and the droid could get the job done.

The droid, now silenced, set about cleansing the cuts and scrapes she had received on her flight down the corridors while making her way to the pros-house in the spaceport. Working as a runner was a dangerous occupation and she hated it, but until now, Kadie had never been the target of the Port Authorities.

Kadie sighed heavily again. Something, or someone, had told them about her efforts to transport illegal BXM parts.

BXMs, illegal transporters used by the drug and pros-keepers to stay one-step ahead of the Authorities, were highly sought after and their pieces were traded on the black market for large sums of credits. She had only agreed to carry the parts to save her ship. That knowledge sat like a heavy stone around her chest, even now.

The droid fussed at her, attempting to pull the shipsuit down her legs. She lifted her butt and allowed it to slide the blood stained cloth away, wincing as she felt layers of skin peeling away with it. Liquid drizzled on her injured skin and she hissed in pain, the sting radiating through her body. She had the coveralls on when she fell, so no grit or dirt got into the soft skin of her knees. She wasn't so sure what she'd find in her hands though and tried to avoid thinking about what she had fallen into on the ground. She knew the filth that coated the ground on the spaceport was legendary for all the wrong reasons. Sometimes it just didn't bear too close an inspection, she told herself.

The droid completed the exam and treatment, professing her ready to go, and Kadie rose painfully from the medi-bed. She set the machine back to sleep mode and hobbled out of the miniscule sickbay toward her cabin. Food was a priority, but a bed for resting more so.

"Computer, alarm in six hours. Prepare a light sustenance pack in six hours ten minutes." She lay down on the hard bed and closed her eyes, pulling the thin covering of the threadbare sheet over her almost nude body.

* * *

A quiet beeping alerted Kadie to the fact that the ship was about to reset. The dark of the room sent a thrill of danger through her for a moment until memories registered. She rose, unsteady as pins and needles shot through her legs, and she swore silently in every shipboard language she knew. Unsurprisingly, this meant quite a few languages were used.

Kadie moved swiftly to the bridge, knowing she needed to stop the system before it locked her down in her cabin, racing faster as the beeping grew louder and more insistent. The door of the bridge opened with a thud as she launched herself toward the command chair, keying in the necessary password and dropping heavily into the seat.

"Override acknowledged," the tinny computer-generated voice announced.

She exhaled in exhaustion while her stomach ached with hunger and her bladder seemed full enough to burst. "Oh well, I guess that should fix it for now. I don't really need sleep, do I?"

She hobbled toward her sanitation room at the back of the bridge, stripping out of the underwear as she made her way slowly through the door. A stop at the toilet, quick sponge bath, and food comprised her immediate plan. The water she used for her sponge bath was frigid. She couldn't afford a heating system, and besides, water in space was a precious commodity, recycled over and again, so anything more she considered a waste. Why spend extra on a luxury she couldn't often use?

Kadie pulled on the panties she had worn before, throwing her towel toward the cabin, where it landed in a heap at the end of the bed.

She'd only had her little ship fifteen months, so funds always seemed tight. In fact, the only other outlay she had made was her medical droid. The craft she could describe as clunky and old with many glitches, but she loved it anyway. It was home, something way outside her previous experience. Ownership, freedom, and belonging were new concepts for her and she smiled wryly at her fierce thoughts.

Stomping to the small kitchen, Kadie pulled out a loaf of bread and a nutritional spread, gray and awful smelling. She sighed. It was the best she could afford, yet full of vitamins and minerals, so she accepted the horrible food without another sound.

Her stomach rumbled as she ate fast, almost choking while wolfing the food down. Two meals a day, especially bread and nutritional spread, wouldn't keep her alive. Kadie knew she needed to find a job soon, but with the Authorities after her, that would be harder to achieve legitimately. A glass of water washed the dry mass down and she cleaned the spartan space, once more thinking over her options.

Nothing easy came to mind as she headed toward the cabin, her knees stiff and aching. Her palms felt hot and her head still ached slightly. She had to ignore the discomfort, as the price of medications was beyond her limited budget and she hoped they wouldn't be necessary. Kadie pulled off her clothing, climbing into her last pair of clean panties and coveralls, shoving the dirty clothing into the small, but half-empty hamper in the corner of the room. She would need to clean them tonight so she had fresh clothing.

Her mind settled to consider her worries. Who had targeted her? Why would anyone want to tell on her?

She'd paid her dues to the port thugs, ensuring she kept in good with them. It meant she had to stretch every credit she made in profit, handling each one with care, paying the invoices that kept arriving, and trying to squirrel enough away to pay the thugs ensuring they left her alone. She knew they went easier on her. She had almost become one of them, living in the squalor of grimy slums which encompassed the port itself. Even so, she still had to pay every lunar month.

She was quiet and careful, paying respect to the pros-keepers who kept her out of trouble on other fronts. In return, they occasionally needed a transfer or some special custom item imported and gave her the job. She tried hard to ensure her rates for them were reasonable. She was small fish, but that didn't change facts. She ran illegal goods back and forth, and if the Authorities found out, Kadie would have even bigger problems.

She sank back down in her seat, downloading the latest reports from Authority and the news-links. Kadie scanned them quickly. She sighed tiredly, letting her head sink back into the seat. She needed to go back, find out what the hell had happened and why. *Shit! I can't give in now.* She fastened her hair back and disengaged the shields. No time like the present, she thought, making the split- second decision. The engines rumbled to life under her hands.

* * *

Jonah got the report of the small Lightbird craft entering the atmosphere. *Oriana's Evadare*, so innocuously named, piloted by one Kadie Frost. She was considered mild and modest, running illicit BXM parts, as well as other small time illegal contraband. The value low enough that it kept her just shy of the Authority's interests.

Her Pilot Association identification listed her as young, barely twenty-four, with red hair, violet eyes, and standing a mere five feet, four inches tall. He had pulled her data off the official Centauri residents list, but it had been sparse. It only named the freighter company she had crewed with at minimum active age of fourteen; he had little to go on. Her parents were listed as unknown, along with her place and date of birth. No known address except her small shuttlecraft.

Jonah headed to the dock, ready to grab her as she left the port, watching the small, tidy, older ship come into a careful landing on Kadie's appointed spot. He waited as the lights winked off on the craft in one quick flash. He continued watching in the silence of the shadows as the night air cooled.

The door cracked open finally and she moved. Her steps were almost soundless down the retractable stairs and across the pavement toward him. He remained still and watchful until she was near him, knowing she hadn't seen him until it was too late. His hand reached out to grab her. He propelled her backward into the dark shadows where he had waited. He thrust a hand over her mouth before she could let out a startled cry. She twisted and turned, trying to escape, but he kept his grip.

"Kadie Frost? You are detained under section seven-one-two of the Centauri judicial code. We have reason to suspect you are running unlawful BXM parts." He got one arm free as she continued her slippery movements, placing small restraints around her wrists as he intoned the words. "You will come with me for questioning."

She squirmed in his grasp, but he let his hands move onto her coverall now, dragging her to a small vehicle he'd stashed near the building. Once there, he checked that the restraints were secure and pushed her into the back seating area, fastening them to a loop with a smooth movements.

He chanced a quick look at her face. Mulishly set lips and cold, staring eyes followed him. Furious, he supposed, at such an easy capture. Her eyes narrowed with anger, but she remained quiet. He chuckled silently, considering her actions to mean she knew it was time to hold her tongue before he came up with any other charges, such as resisting restraint.

He whistled as he climbed into the vehicle he had hidden away and allowed it to slowly rise in the air.

* * *

Kadie dropped her aching head into her hot and stinging hands as they rested on her knees in the cell. The pounding rhythm in her head had become worse the longer she had been there.

Damn, I thought I had been cautious by using the small, handheld radar to watch for anyone around. Why didn't it work? How did the Authority man manage to find her? He must have a blocker, which is why I didn't see his signature on the radar.

Kadie sniffed. Until now, she'd always managed to avoid capture when breaking any laws. *It's my bad luck I got caught this time.* Carrying the BXM parts was such a mistake, but *he* said they would change the ownership records if she didn't do it.

She sighed as the thoughts swirled. *I should have gone to see Old Nevin when the problem first arose.*

The man that arrested her, Captain Jonah Fielding, she had heard of. A straight man, everyone agreed. He didn't associate with the old, corrupt Authorities. But at this point that was cold comfort. *How can I possibly explain that I have nothing else except my little Oriana's Evadare and that's why I took the chance?* Her stomach rebelled and she dry heaved right there in the cells as catcalls and laughter from other prisoners filled the air. Thank the Lights at least I got put in a single cell. Her head ached brutally and she wavered slightly, waiting for Captain Fielding to send for her.

"Kadie Frost? Captain Fielding wants to see you." The clank of the cell door told her someone was coming; she struggled to her feet, lifting tired, sore eyes.

A young man, little more than a boy really, with a freshly pressed uniform marched in, unfastened her from the restraint loop, and pulled her out the door and into an anonymous corridor.

Hoots and hollers met her ears as she allowed herself to be paraded down the long walkway. As if cattle in a mooncow yard, she thought, closing her eyes as the Authority man pulled her toward a heavy, metal door at the end of the corridor. He stopped there and she opened her eyes, reading the sign on the door.

Interrogation Room One. What a great name, she thought snidely. Really inventive.

The door opened slowly and she was quickly thrust inside. The door snapped shut behind her as she looked around the bare room. A table and two chairs sat, scarred and ugly, in the middle of the floor. The metal was cold and glittering in the cool air as the air circulators pushed currents around the frigid room. She made her way over and sat down, waiting for the captain to enter. Her head drooped to the table and she let it rest, seeking the refreshing cool on her overly hot skin.

Her hands stung and her eyes burned. She felt sorry for herself as she thought about the mess she had gotten into, and she turned her stinging hands to check the damage. They were bright red and radiated heat. The deep scratches were swollen and weepy; sticky drops of goop coated the raw skin. Never a good sign, she already knew that.

"Kadie Frost?"

She started. Obviously, the woolly, heavy feeling in her head had overtaken her and she had dropped off to sleep as she waited. Her skin burned against the metal tabletop in the coolness of the room.

"That's me." Her head hurt viciously, but now she realized her throat burned too.

"Captain Fielding is my name. I believe you and I can discuss BXM parts?" He lifted an eyebrow and she noted the captain had the most amazing blue eyes she had ever seen, teamed with long, black hair fastened at the back of his neck, high cheeks, and impossibly chiseled features. He had full, pink lips that would make a woman cry when they moved over hers. Huh? Where did that thought come from?

She blinked, dazed by the thought, and considered her plan of attack. "What? Oh, the BXM parts." She swallowed and felt the razor blades she was sure were in her neck slashing from the inside which then proceeded to burn. "They aren't mine. They never were."

"Right, you are doing a favor for someone else." His voice was dry and loud to her aching head, but she nodded, willing him to understand her predicament.

"Yeah. I can't tell you who they belong to though. I don't know their name." She should confess everything now. The truth might get her out of this mess, she thought.

"Ms. Frost. *Kadie.* Can I be candid with you?" He leaned

forward in his seat, his eyes watching her face. "You're being framed in my estimation. I want to help you. I really do, but you have to help me too."

Sure, sure. I've heard those words before. "I'm a social service droid and it is my role to help you." She'd heard that as a child in the slums more than once. Just look where that led to. No one is trustworthy on Centauri.

"I'm telling the truth. I don't know whose they are. I don't remember the woman who approached me." Captain Fielding sat opposite Kadie at the table, and she let her gaze slide away from his face. It could make angels weep, she thought.

"Kadie, tell me where you made the deal then. We might be able to get something from the location."

Damn, how can I tell him I did the deal in the dirtiest pros-house on Centauri? Her thoughts startled her. Since when did she care if someone knew she associated with the pros- workers? They did a decent night's work for decent credit...usually, anyway. "I don't..."

"You don't remember. Yeah, I've heard that song before." He pulled a disk from his pocket, slapping it on the table between them. "This is the list of the parts you were found carrying before you took off."

She looked at him and then the disk.

* * *

Jonah watched her, sitting listlessly in the seat. Her skin as pale as death, and she was sweating like she was coming off a three-day drunk, he thought humorlessly. She watched him suspiciously, as if he wasn't to be trusted. The ID hadn't told him of her quiet voice or that her pink lips could make him hot enough to self-combust. It hadn't warned him that she had a lithe body, rounded nicely in the right places under the shapeless coverall she wore. It sure as hell didn't tell him that he would feel the need to reach out and touch her baby-fine skin or mold her body to his either.

He swore silently in his head. He knew the deal had occurred in the Silver Squirrel Pros-house. So why wouldn't she tell him that? Was she moonlighting as a pros, perhaps? The thought had his stomach churning. It wasn't one that sat very well with him.

"What in hell were you doing in the Silver Squirrel anyway?" He regretted the words instantly, watching fascinated as frustration rose. She flinched slightly, and he felt sick. A ruddy glow crept up her neck toward her cheeks. The blush color against the pallor of her face made him frown slightly, answering his silent question. Something more might be going on there, but she wasn't a pros. He knew it instinctively, and his uneasiness about the whole situation deepened.

"I don't..." She coughed, eyes closing, and he thought for a minute she was either a damn good actress or something was wrong. That glitter in her eyes when they reopened, almost glassy, alerted him that something was definitely very wrong.

"Ms. Frost? Kadie? Are you unwell?" He wanted to round the corner of the table, but rules were rules. He had to stay on his side, but he wanted to get up and go to her. His hands itched to check, but he controlled his emotions. Jonah shoved determined hands in his pockets and waited.

"I'll be fine." She didn't sound well, he thought.

"Kadie, I'll be frank. I believe you are being framed and I think I can help you, while you help in solving the case."

Her head snapped up and her eyes narrowed. "You want an informer." Her words were as cold as the polar icecaps on Neptune and, for an instant, he wondered if she would refuse.

"Yes. Essentially that is what I want." He nodded and waited.

"Why me?"

"Why not you? You need help, and I can offer that." He watched her wavering in front of him. He knew she fully understood, or at least enough to not look a gift horse in the mouth. This gift horse wanted to help get her out of trouble with the Authorities.

She was searching for a loophole, he thought, watching her face for a hint that didn't exist. She really had a poker face, nothing showed except in her eyes, if you watched intently. She wanted something that would get her out of the trouble she was currently in and he was damned sure he knew a way to achieve that.

"What do I get?" She whispered the words so quietly he had to bend forward to hear them.

"We can make this whole charge go away. We can help you with the troubles you are obviously having. You just need to tell me what I need to know."

She sighed heavily and he knew he had her. The way her slight shoulders slumped, the shaky hand that rose to her forehead.

"You can make them leave me alone? I just want to fly my ship and run freight." Her words were tight.

"Okay. We can do that, but what can you tell me?"

She lifted her head enough for him to see her eyes roll back as she slumped to the floor in a dead faint.

* * *

God! Her head ached and she was sore all over. She tried to roll, but found herself restrained.

"Where am I?" She opened her eyes and there was the current bane of her life, Captain Jonah Fielding. The floor was cold and she shivered; her body burning and on fire.

"You passed out in the interrogation room. I have medics on their way." He leaned over her, and even with her roiling stomach and sore head, she saw the concern in his eyes and that clean smell of him filled her senses.

"I don't need a medic." She struggled against his hands.

"Yes, you do. Now lie still."

"I can't afford a medic." She mumbled the words. She hated admitting she had next to nothing. The small amount of control she had over her life was continuously stripped away by being poor and close to destitute. She hated that.

"It's okay—"

"No, it isn't okay. I don't have any credits to pay. I can't afford a medic." She spat the words at him and struggled weakly once more.

"You don't have to. The department takes care of the bill." The concern in his eyes made her sad. She could only dream of meeting a man like this. So good and clean and, from what she had heard, honest.

Kadie had already summed him up as the door opened and an older man, overweight with a receding hairline and an overbite of immense proportions, stood in the doorway puffing as his eyes moved from side to side. He wiped sweat from his reddened cheeks, waiting for the door to open fully. In his pudgy hands he carried a large bag and she watched as he bumbled into the room.

"Sorry it took so long, Captain. Now let's have a look." He crouched close to Kadie.

The smell of stale sweat assaulted her and she dry heaved once more. A cold hand touched her forehead and she yelped, pulling away and knocking her head hard on the unyielding surface. A pain shot through her head and she moaned.

"That's it. You aren't well. You need to go to the infirmary." The captain's words echoed through her brain.

"No, I can't afford it." The thin wail erupted from her lips and she saw his mouth tighten.

That wouldn't be covered by the department. Infirmaries

cost lots of credits, so do the medications they dispense. Credits I just don't have. "I can go back to *Oriana's Evadare.*" She watched his hair swinging as he shook his head.

"No, it's been impounded until we deal with the issue of the BXM parts. I have it on lock-down right now."

She jerked. He had said nothing about that, and she felt sick that she had been about to agree to his proposition. A wave of dizziness swept through her body, and that cold feeling that comes with nausea assailed her once more.

"My ship. You can't do that!" She wanted to fight him, but her limbs were heavy, her head aching in time to the pulsing of her body, and her stomach revolted.

"I can and I did. Now what are we going to do with you? I can't have you here, infected and sick, with the rest of the prisoners. It's also clear you can't go to the infirmary." He stopped, and she watched as he thought. "You'll have to come home with me." His words were final.

She closed her eyes as the darkness washed over her again.

Chapter Two

Jonah shook his head. He didn't know what had come over him to suggest taking this woman into his home, though at least her threat value was minimal. However, here he was, with a very ill woman in his arms as he strode into the elevator of his level five, secured housing block.

She was light, and burning up. The medic trotted behind him, puffing and panting, red faced from exertion. Jonah punched the button and keyed in the password that told the elevator who it was. *I hope he doesn't have a cardiac arrest,* Jonah thought. *I can't handle another patient and I surely couldn't lift him off the floor if he did.* He shook his head at the unkind thoughts, reminding himself it was the man within that mattered.

There was a whoosh as the elevator rose through the building to the fortieth floor.

Jonah had bought the building with the money his parents bequeathed him, though he only lived on one floor, renting the rest out to corporate and residential tenants. Really, he didn't have to work, but loved what he did and he knew he was damned good at his job. It was one of the major reasons the Centauri government had sought him out specifically from the busy moon base where he had previously been in charge of security, to fix their systemic issues.

The doors opened into the living area. He hadn't wanted luxurious or richly furnished and had settled for simple and homelike; the cool air within the room washed over pale, wood furnishings and muted colors. It was relaxing to his tired eyes, but today he didn't stop to soak up the atmosphere, instead he strode through the room to the first door on the right. The guest bedroom had been unused until now. He busied himself laying the woman on the bed and then waited for the medic to set up the necessary medical equipment he needed. The modular IV pole sat beside the bed and he watched as the medic pushed the needle into her arm.

"She has a high-grade fever. You will need to watch that it doesn't climb higher. Bathe her with warm water to make her feel comfortable. Not cold. You need to ring me immediately if she gets worse." He took a swab from her mouth and a sample of blood from her arm, running them through the medi-scanner, and nodded to himself, putting his equipment into a small bag.

"What do I do if she doesn't wake up soon?" They left the room, heading for the elevator.

"She will, I guarantee, very soon. Get her to take these tablets with food and make her rest." The medic stood in front of the elevator. "Now, how do I get out of here?"

Jonah hit the button and the door opened. He preset it for the first floor, using his passcode, and watched as the door closed behind the medic.

Jonah wandered back into the bedroom, looking at the small woman on the bed as he leaned against the doorjamb. She lay still, and he let his eyes travel over her. He took in the durable but well-worn coverall, noting it was clean despite its threadbare appearance; the choppy-edged, red hair; and the fine bone structure of her face. She lived tight, he thought. He had never lived like that. There was no way he could appreciate the difficulties for a young girl on her own with no one to fall back on.

After a while, Jonah pushed away from the door, standing upright, and made his way to the kitchen to prepare a coffee for himself.

* * *

Softness beneath her. Something in her arm, restricting her movements, hurting slightly.

She must have moaned her discomfort. "Stay still." The voice penetrated the dark and she opened her eyes. Muted light shone overhead and she turned her head away from it. Captain Fielding.

"Where in hell am I?" The words escaped and she wanted to wince. What a way to win friends and influence people.

"You are in my home, Kadie. Now lie still."

She struggled to rise and felt a hand on her chest pushing her back down.

"I'm no pros, Captain. I don't put out, so don't think you can handle me." She knew what would come next. He would put on the 'See what I did for you, now you do for me' lines, but instead he just jerked back at her words, as if she had smacked him in the face. His eyes held hurt and she felt a pang of regret at her hasty words. But it was the only way she knew to survive intact in her cold, hard world.

"I know you're not a pros, Kadie. It's okay. I certainly don't wish to handle you." He bit the words out and she cringed.

He had helped her, brought her into his home, and she

had just thrown it back in his face. *Great work, Kadie. Now watch him throw you out on your dumbass rear.* She closed her eyes, swallowing hard against the lump of fear that lodged there. After all, her ship was locked down. So where was she going to go? She was sick, which meant she needed medicines. Something she couldn't afford.

"I'm sorry." The words slipped out quietly.

"Do you feel hungry?"

"No. But thank you." She felt tears leaking from her closed eyes.

The bed dipped. "Look, I know you aren't feeling so great, but I need to know, who did you deliver the parts to?"

"I didn't. I was picking them up. They were left at the Silver Squirrel for me to take to Harvest Moon. I was supposed to deliver them to the Pros-house there." The words slipped quietly from her lips and she wanted to cry. She only agreed to run BXM parts from one lousy pros-house to another on a dirty moon colony where the worst criminals were known to hang out, because she had no choice.

"Why, Kadie? Why did you agree? You don't strike me as the sort of woman who participates in that sort of thing." His words were quiet in the silent room.

"I'm not. They said if I didn't, they would alter the ownership records of my ship. I have nothing else. It's all I have." Her voice cracked.

* * *

Her words had wounded him, but he could see they were her shield, a cloak she wore to protect herself from the world. Jonah settled himself on the bed next to her. "Who are they, and why would they want to alter the ownership records?" Even as he spoke, he placed a hand on her forehead, judging her fever to have dropped slightly.

"I don't know who they are. No one says their names at the port, but we know about them. They wield power and have fingers in every pie. You name it, they can do it. They wanted me to take the BXM parts to the pros-house. I know the girls at the Silver Squirrel, so there are never any questions when I come and go. I know there are some dirty deals going down there, but I stay out of them. Everyone there knows I don't deal in dirty parts." She stopped and he watched her swallow. "They did it to one of the other ship owners recently. They changed the ownership records and then evicted him from his ship when it was sold." She shrugged weakly.

He deduced she was running out of energy. "Wait here, and I'll get you a bowl of soup."

She shook her head, trying to rise. "I need to go to the bathroom."

"Oh." He hadn't considered that she had needs, but watched bemused as she struggled to rise, popping the canula from her arm with a short yelp. "Right through there." He pointed to a doorway and she followed his finger. "Do you need help?"

She looked at him soberly. "I haven't ever had help. But thank you." She unsteadily made for the door, closing it in his face.

He sat back down on the bed to wait for her. The running water sounds told him it was time to move. He waited until she slowly made her way back to the bed before heading to the kitchen. A hearty soup and maybe a roll, something easily digestible and nutritious would be best.

He rooted around in the kitchen, finding one frozen soup and then a second he had ordered in. He found fresh rolls in the refrigerator and was heating the soup when a sound caught his attention. She stood by the wall, pale but beautiful, in the fading light of day.

"You should be in bed."

"I don't do bed well. Would you like me to help in some way?" Her words were whisper soft and her eyes dark, though she at least had a hint of pink in her cheeks now. He watched as she walked lightly and he motioned to the seats.

"Sit down and wait then."

She perched on the edge of the chair, uncertain of her welcome. His heart bled a little for the waif she must have been.

"Why are you alone?"

"My parents ditched me when I was, I don't know...maybe six or seven. They worked freighters and came here for some reason or other, probably a load, though I honestly don't remember it all that well. Anyway, I think I was just another mouth and there were others, younger than me, to think of. At least two, or even three, from what I can remember. They sent me to the port for something and when I came back, they were gone." She shrugged lightly.

A cold feeling sliced through his belly. How could someone abandon a child like that? "How did you manage then?"

She closed her eyes. "Ahh, you want all my secrets." She smiled briefly, but it was cold and brittle. "Okay then. For the first few years, I hid in drains and stole food and clothing. The slums have many places to hide and I got to know them well. Then a social services droid found me, pinned me, and put me into one of the juvie hostels. I learned lots about abuse, how to fight, and most of all, how to survive. I also made sure I got an education. I busted out when I was about fourteen and found work on a freighter. Haven't really thought about it since then. That was about ten years ago. Once I had work, I stopped living the rough way and have done it honestly in the last few years."

"Have you searched for your parents?" Hearing her words, his heart ached for her, but he needed to know.

"No. They didn't want me. Now, all I could be is a meal ticket, so I don't want that lump of space stone to deal with." She shrugged nonchalantly, or so she no doubt thought. But the sadness in her eyes lingered.

The soup was bubbling over and he scooped it up. God, what must it have been like for her? He couldn't understand her life. There was no comparison to his, with loving parents and his much younger sisters.

"Don't feel sorry for me. I could have given up, taken to crime. I didn't though. I wanted to be my own person, to be proud of my achievements, and to be someone." She must have caught a flash of his roiling emotions.

The words stopped him in his tracks. Wasn't that, after all, what he had done? Become someone in his own right? Except, his path had been easier.

He poured the soup into bowls and placed them on the table. He watched as she inhaled the spicy scent of the light meal. She ate slowly, breaking her roll up to mop the bottom of the dish at the end. She closed her eyes and sighed with completion while he studied her.

"So, how long have you lived in this building? I know you're new to the job here on Centauri. They talk about you down at the port. It must be great to live in this comfort." She opened her eyes and waited for his answer.

"I've been on Centauri for about fifteen months. I like it. This apartment suits me, not too big or small. Not too shiny either."

She nodded her head at his words, giving him the impression she tried to understand what he meant.

He stretched out a hand, holding a foil packet. "Anyway, you need to take this tablet and then head to bed. I have a day off tomorrow, so we can do something about grabbing clothes from your ship then."

She smiled. "Yeah, probably wouldn't hurt." She had a funny look on her face though as she stood and headed to the bedroom door. "Thank you for letting me stay. I will repay you somehow." Then she turned quietly and was gone.

* * *

She woke, the softness at her back surprising for an instant as she bolted upright, looking around. The room was comfortable with a chair, dresser, and even a mirror above a small table. Nothing like her usual bunk on *Oriana's Evadare* and that worried her. It took a moment for the events of yesterday to filter through her mind. Captain Fielding had brought her home when she collapsed in front of him at the Authority headquarters, then she had told him her history over a bowl of soup. She groaned, thinking over what she had disclosed. Every freaking detail she vividly remembered.

"Well, my girl, time to head back where you belong, which sure isn't here." She crawled out of the bed, pulling the slightly grimy coverall back on, and hurried to the clean modular bathroom. She washed her face, luxuriating in the warm water that she didn't get on her ship, before heading into the lounge area. It was empty, and she hunted for a notepad and pen. Spying one on the desk, she simply wrote, *Thanks for all the help. I'll pay you back when I can.*

She hurried toward the elevator, pressed the down button, and waited for it to open. Her feet tapped a quick tattoo on the shiny floor as she waited impatiently. Kadie wanted to be out of there before he got up and saw her. She really didn't do pity very well and that is the reaction she was sure he had exuded the night before.

The ding sounded through the apartment and she hurried in, pressing on the close door button. Nothing happened. She pressed the button again, a little more agitated this time. Damn, how did she get this thing to work? A movement heralded his entry to the room and she groaned silently as he came in, seeing her standing in the elevator and raising an eyebrow. Her stomach churned at what he must think she was doing.

"You need the pass-code for it to work." The words were dry and she felt like five types of idiot standing in the open elevator. "Were you planning on going somewhere?" He watched closely and she knew she blushed, feeling the heat rising on her skin.

"Damn. I was going to get out of your hair. You've been great and all, but you know? I need to go back where I belong." She looked around. "And this isn't it." She glanced back at him, waiting for him to enter the pass-code, but he stood watching her for a moment, then shook his head before wandering into the kitchen.

She was perplexed. He could have his space back, she would be out of his hair, and life would go on pretty much as before. What could possibly be wrong with that? Except *Oriana's Evadare* is still in lock-down. She scowled at the errant thought.

She could hear him puttering around in the kitchen and moved forward.

"Coffee?" he asked brightly.

She stared at him. What was he doing? Hadn't she made herself clear?

"Umm, Captain Fielding? We both know I need to get out of here. I don't belong here. So how about you let me out, and I'll go without interrupting your life any further?"

He turned with a frown on his face. "No. You are here until I am ready to let you go. Which isn't yet. So be a good guest and tell me if you prefer tea or coffee."

This is so out of my league. The thought filtered through her mind. "Coffee." She muttered the word as he stood watching her. "No cream or sugar."

This whole setup was alien to her and when he reappeared with the cup, she took her coffee, sipping it slowly, inhaling the taste of the dark roasted beans as she stood in a corner of the immaculate and well appointed kitchen. The muck she usually drank could never be called coffee after this, she told herself silently. But then, what else could you call reconstituted dishwater? Because, honestly, that was the best description for it.

He motioned toward a large glass window and she followed slowly as he opened it up to reveal a hidden balcony. "Come on, join me on the balcony and we can watch the world go by." She got as far as the door and her stomach dipped.

Kadie stepped back, nearly dropping the coffee. "I...I can't. It's too high." She backtracked to the kitchen and heard him follow.

"Kadie, I'm sorry. I didn't mean to freak you out." He reached for her hand as she stood quivering in his kitchen, silent tears running down her face. He touched her and she broke down. Big, noisy sobs escaped her, shaking her body.

"They used to threaten to hold us out the windows until we did what they wanted. At the hostel, the adults used to make us do things, running goods from the pros houses, messages, and some even had to have sex. I never did the sex thing, but they used to have me run errands in the pros houses. I knew most of the girls in the pros houses, so I usually got that job 'cause they would let me in." She stifled a sob and sniffled. "I thought I was over my fear of heights." She wailed the last words miserably, embarrassment following swiftly on the heels of her outburst.

He wound a strong arm around her shoulder, pulling her

in close, and she could smell him again. So clean and crisp, and she felt dirty and grimy. Just like the ragged child she had been, living on the streets. No matter how she tried, it was hard to get past the hurt she still felt now that he knew about her past, but she soaked up the comfort he offered anyway.

* * *

Jonah held her. Dear God, she was soft and so sad. He just wanted to make her feel better.

He pulled her close, feeling her delicate body curl against his. No matter how hard she thought she imagined herself to be, she needed holding and soothing. That much he could do for her.

He dropped his chin to the top of her head. Kadie's smooth, red hair was like a halo, and he bent to kiss her cheek. She made a whisper of a sound and turned her head toward him. He closed his eyes. Her violet eyes had struck him to the core. So hurt and bruised that he ached again for the young girl who had lived such a terrible childhood. He carefully led her to the seats far away from the window, holding her close to him, while her subtle fragrance battered his senses.

She was beautiful, but so thoroughly damaged from her life so far. He had this urgent need to make her feel better, to see her laugh, and to watch her eyes sparkle. He shook himself mentally though. They had two days for him to build enough of a bond that she would help him close the case. He shouldn't forget what he needed to achieve.

This wasn't doing the job, he told himself firmly, but his heart and body wanted to rail against his head.

She sniffled and he noted her crying jag was ending while he internally tussled with his emotions and his own body's needs.

Jonah grabbed some tissues from the box. He knew they were also a luxury and she would be wary, but he handed them over anyway, watching as she wiped away the residue of her tears.

"I don't usually lose it like that." She hiccupped slightly as she said the words in a husky, just-finished-crying voice.

"I didn't think you did. Look, let's start again, shall we? Hi. My name is Jonah. Pleased to meet you." He gravely held out his hand, and a shy smile edged to the side of her lips as she took it. She still seemed wary, but accepted his hand. Jonah noted the calluses on her hands, as if she'd labored hard in her past.

"Hi, Jonah. I'm Kadie."

He smiled. First step accomplished. "Let's go see about grabbing you some clothes from your ship." He watched as she turned beet red.

"Um, about that. I don't have any clean clothes on the ship. I was planning on doing the laundry today, but, well...I didn't get a chance." She released a pent-up breath and he smiled.

"Okay, no problem, let me see what I have in my wardrobe." He stopped still, noting the surprise and a flash of fire in her eyes. He knew what was racing through her mind. What kind of man keeps clothes that are suitable for a woman just lying around? He smiled broadly before continuing. "I have some of my sisters' clothes here." He led the way into a bedroom decorated in pale tones of green.

He grabbed the doors of the wardrobe and yanked them open. She fell back with a cry. He turned to see surprise on her face. "What's the matter?"

"You have so many clothes."

He smiled at the shock in her voice.

"Well, they aren't all mine. I have two younger sisters who like to visit. See?" He pointed to piles of clothing, obviously in smaller sizes than his. He reached out and grabbed a shirt. "Try this on." He turned back and rooted around for some bottoms. Maybe the loose, leisure-wear pants would be best, he thought.

He turned around, only to see the stunning sight of her already pulling off the coverall and standing in front of him in panties and bra, pulling on the t-shirt he had passed her. His mouth dried as her beautifully formed breasts, about the size of ripe grapefruit jiggled slightly and there was a coil of heat low in his belly. Her panties barely covered any part her. In fact, he thought they were just this side of legal. They were nearly see-through and the red thatch of hair he could spy through them called like a siren to his sight. His blood heated further.

She pulled the shirt down as far as she could, but it was too small, molding over her breasts so that they stood out, ripe and enticing. She was stripping it off when she noticed him watching.

"What?"

"You are so beautiful." He felt like a schoolboy, a massive erection in his shorts at the sight of her nearly naked form. Her nipples tightened under his gaze, pebbling erotically, and he knew she watched him as her eyes grew heavy under his gaze. He reached out and she stepped into his arms.

"I don't usually do this sort of thing, you know." She whispered the words against his mouth as he crushed her lips to his.

Chapter Three

It hadn't occurred to Kadie that Jonah would be so turned on watching her dress, until his eyes started smoldering. In that instant, she was on fire for him.

The heat that grew in her belly turned her body to melting liquid and she could feel herself growing damp between her thighs. The shirt he had worn this morning fit tightly against his body, outlining the ridges and curves of his chest. His bottoms hid little she thought, noticing the outline of his erection with a sharp intake of breath.

His lips touched hers and she could taste the coffee he'd had earlier. His hands were firm against her body, but not cruel, and she arched into them as they lightly skated over her bare skin. They slid slowly down and he pulled away from her mouth. The mute question Kadie answered as she took one firm hand and placed it on her breast. Yes. She wanted this union.

Jonah's touch was electric and she burned beneath his knowing fingers. He swooped in for another kiss. Scorching her with heat and crushing her lower body against his, tongues of fire licked everywhere their bodies met.

"Oh God." His voice was hoarse, and desire flashed through her. He deepened the kiss, thrusting his tongue into her mouth as she let her hands move over his chest, feeling the firm muscles beneath her questing fingers.

His hand slipped down the back of her panties. They offered no real barrier, and his fingers kneaded her backside. He pulled her closer into the cradle of his thighs. His hands pulled her panties down over her hips and they dropped to the floor, forgotten as his mouth ravaged hers.

Kadie's heart thrummed against her ribs, and when Jonah pulled away, she sucked in an unsteady breath, her legs shaking as his strong arms lifted her. The movement startled her and she opened drugged, heavy eyes. The softness of the bed below her was a shock to her system as he gently laid her on the well cushioned mattress.

"Tell me you want this." He growled the words and she watched, fascinated as his face turned hard with lust.

Mutely, she opened her legs and pulled him closer to her. She knew he could smell her arousal, wet and musky, in the air as she reached up, and his shaking hands reached behind to unclasp her bra.

He slipped the straps down and left her breasts free to his gaze. His unsteady hand rose to cup one, grazing her sensitive nipple. She cried out, throwing her head back and closing her eyes as the sensation rocketed through her shaking body.

The hot wetness of his mouth surprised her as it clasped tightly over the nub, and the feel of his tongue moving over her skin took her breath away as he suckled.

"Jonah? I want you so badly, I'm shaking with it."

He lifted his head, and she could see the lust shining in his eyes. She panted, reaching for him, and as he came closer, she grasped the bottom of his shirt, pulling at it with jerky movements. She needed to see all of him; her body demanded the touch of his skin against her aroused flesh.

Jonah took over, grabbing the bottom of the shirt from her inept fingers, tearing it in his rush to pull it over his head. Her hands were at the band of his pants, pushing at his body. He brushed the pants away and his engorged shaft sprang free from the confines of the material. The tip glistened with the sweat that coated his body. Magnificent!

His chest was hairless, his body a sculpture of muscles. The look in his eyes when she checked his face took away whatever breath she had left. Heaven!

Kadie reached for him, touching his skin, and he experienced the explosion of fire, she could tell in the way he jerked under her soft touch.

Jonah crept up the bed, stretching out a hand and pushing on her shoulder so that she reclined. Her legs opened further as he settled himself. "God, I want you. I want to be filling you all the way." His eyes shone as he touched her intimately, tracing fingers along her cleft, and she arched up, muscles tight and ready for him.

His fingers played over her skin, sinking slowly between the soft folds, dipping and then pulling back. Each touch wound her tighter. She could feel the wetness on his fingertips with each provoking move. This time, though, his fingers pushed through the entry to her core and didn't pull back. This time when they slipped within, she gloried in the intrusion, so thick and hard, pushing within her body, moving as she moaned her pleasure.

She cracked her eyes open a little and could see him. His other hand had grabbed his cock. Just holding. Oh my God! She'd never seen anything so erotic.

Kadie placed her own hand on top of his, pushing it away, grasping his cock firmly, pumping gently in rhythm with his movements.

His thumb played with the small nub between her legs and each touch sent a zing through her body. Once more she arched beneath him, mindless need riding her hard, while her heart pounded.

"I need you. Inside me." The words were hoarse as they ripped from her mouth.

He stopped and moved his hand, slowly and purposefully settled between her legs, the head of his erection just at the entrance to her core.

She could feel her dampness as she levered herself up, bending her knees so that he could enter her with a slow slide. The blunt head pushed, and her body opened to allow him entrance. He flexed his hips and slid a little deeper, the ripples of sensation pulling at her as she felt his movements.

He thrust again, just a small sliding movement, and she gasped, feeling him flush against her.

Beneath him, she undulated her hips, no more than a nudge, but the electricity surged through her again while her nipples rubbed against his hard, satiny chest. Each rasp urging her closer to him and to the shattering climax she needed so badly. His movements grew faster, thrusting himself within her and she met them, stroke for stroke, as the sound of sighs and groans filled the air, mingling with the musky scent of sex.

The pleasure burst over her. Spasms and tremors shook her while he pumped, gripping her hips while he pistoned back and forth, before finally tipping his head back. The muscles in his neck corded as he spilled into her. The scorching heat of his release filled her as he groaned one last time. "Kadie."

She laid still, her heart thudding in her chest. What in God's name had she done?

* * *

Kadie stiffened in his arms. Oh God! They shouldn't have had sex. She was an informant and he was the Captain of Authority. It shouldn't have happened. It had, though, and it was the greatest sex of his life.

He closed his eyes, rolled onto his back, and put a weary arm over his eyes. She lay still in his arms. He could hear her breath, feel the pounding rhythm of her heart, and knew his was beating like a drum, trying to thud its way out of his chest.

"Kadie...I..." What should he say? What could he say?

"It's okay. We both wanted it." The words were small and he felt like a creep. She was still recovering, looking for clothes, and he had just gone at her like a rutting beast. He thought about her words, she didn't do this sort of thing.

He could tell she was still quite innocent. She had been so tight when he had filled her. But her responses had set him on fire. Truthfully, she had fired him up in a way he had never before experienced.

"Maybe, but I shouldn't—"

Kadie lifted a hand, laying a soft finger across his lips. "Don't. Please don't say you're sorry. It was fabulous, but we can't do this again. We are different. I'm from the slums and you belong here. I'm on the wrong side of the law, and you enforce it. It can't be. We can't be." She slowly moved, edging away, and he moved his arm, cracked open an eye, and watched.

She clambered out of the bed, grabbed her panties and bra, pulling them on in economical movements, and picked up her coverall.

He frowned. "What are you doing?"

"I can't stay here. I have to go back to where I belong." The words hung in the air between them.

"You can't go." He let the words drop, like heavy stones. She was sick, he had just had the best sex of his life, and he felt something for her. No way was she going anywhere.

"Look, Jonah. We've already ascertained I'm not lily-white. I know how to survive and move on, and that's what I'm doing right now. You can't keep me here, because it would be wrong. You and I both know that. If you feel that badly, find me somewhere in the slums to stay. Hell, I'll even stay at the pros-house if they have a spare room."

Her breath hitched and his chest ached at her words. "I'll even promise not to leave the pros-house until you say I can. But don't go imagining that just because we had sex, we have anything with permanence attached. It was sex. Right? Great sex, but still, that's all."

He stared at her. *That was all?* Who did she think she was kidding with that statement? He was willing to bet everything he owned that no one in his group of friends had ever experienced anything so mind blowing.

She turned back to the bed and looked him straight in the eye. "You have a mighty fine body, and are great at using it, but I need to go. Now. Without complicating the situation any further."

He closed his eyes. Something in his chest shrivelled and he rolled out of the bed. If that was how she wanted it, then fine. The sharp edge of anger roared that he didn't care. "Where do you want me to take you? Not the Silver Squirrel."

"No, take me to The Light House. The girls know me, and they can find me a bed for a few days. I also need to get to *Oriana's Evadare* and grab some clothes. I can arrange to wash them at the pros house."

"I'll organize that. Do you need anything else?" He reached out for the pants and shirt he had lost in the heat of passion, grimacing as he saw the tear in his t-shirt and reached for another out of the open cupboard.

"No." She turned away as he pulled on the clothes, found shoes, thrust them onto his bare feet, and grabbed his identity disks. He motioned to the doorway and she wandered through and around the corner.

Inside, his stomach churned with guilt. She couldn't get out of there fast enough and that didn't make him feel any better. She hurried into the bedroom she had used, picked up her scuffed boots, jammed them on, and scurried to the elevator. They stepped in and he entered the pass-code without a word.

* * *

Shit! She'd hurt his feelings. But, damn it all, she was scared. She felt so much more; the intensity of the emotions frightened her. She felt miserable and confused even with the afterglow of the best sex of her life.

He led the way silently to the vehicle and she trudged behind him, jumping in. He slammed the accelerator. The drive to the Light House was silent. He dodged and wove his way through the crowds of people and pulled up with a slam outside. The bouncer, a big, burly, hairless guy with yellow eyes, moved forward.

"Hey Joe, can you watch the car?" The words slipped out, and when she looked at Jonah's face she could tell he wasn't happy. She didn't need a translator to work out he was cross that she'd spoken to the bouncer. Or that she knew him by name. Kadie sighed. They walked to the door, which Jonah opened. Here was a gentleman. It was unusual in this area of the port. The thought rose unbidden and she had to swipe away the tear that formed in her eye, hoping he hadn't seen it.

The madam, Della, descended, looking from Jonah to Kadie and back. She obviously knew who he was. "Captain? Can I help you?" Della eyeballed Kadie, and then swung back to Jonah. Kadie swallowed audibly.

"Kadie needs somewhere to stay. Can you help her out?"

Della's face turned white. "What happened? Kadie? Did they find you?" The words slipped out of Della's mouth and Kadie closed her eyes for a second, wishing she hadn't said that. She so didn't want to go there. Didn't need Jonah to understand that they, the ones she was hiding from, were hunting for her.

"Did who find you? Kadie?" He turned a hard stare on her and she wanted to sink through the floor.

"No one." Her poor attempt at evasion failed and her stomach flip flopped as he whipped a hand around, grabbing her as she made to head upstairs.

"Who?" The word was firm and cold.

"Them. They call themselves the Consortium."

He stared at the madam, waiting for more and Kadie was sure she'd fall through a crack in the floor. Silence stretched until the madam grunted and pointed at Jonah.

Della huffed and shook her head. "The ones in charge of all the smuggling. The ones who steal ships and use those who can't protect themselves. Like Kadie, here."

Kadie wound her fingers in the material of the shirt, knowing that he wouldn't settle for anything less than everything but unwilling to tell him herself.

"They want Kadie and her ship. She didn't realize when she bought it that it was one they had changed the docs for before, and she picked it up for a song. She refused to sell it back, so they went after her." Della's voice softened. "Kadie's a good girl, Captain. She tries to do the right thing, and I've known her for a long time. She wouldn't have done anything wrong."

"Is that true, Kadie? Have they been chasing you since you bought *Oriana's Evadare?*" Jonah's voice demanded an answer. He wanted a truthful answer at that, without any evasions or half facts.

"Yeah." Unless she told him everything, he wouldn't leave

her alone. But damn, she didn't want him pitying her. That was the last thing she needed right now.

"Right, then you will have to stay with me. Is there any more I need to know?" He turned his attention back to Della, holding onto Kadie's arm in a bruising grip. Kadie squirmed against the hold and Della raised one perfectly plucked eyebrow. The garnet of her gown and the red hair made her look like a flame-haired temptress on those stairs as it molded to her impossibly trim figure.

For years, Della had been the top girl, and when the last madam retired, Della had taken over. The girls of The Light House had to meet her stringent standards of figure, hygiene, and education. Della had even approached Kadie, but it wasn't the life she had wanted, so the rebuff had been accepted with good humor.

"They came last night looking for Kadie. They saw the ship was in her spot before it was impounded, so they knew she was back. They also heard she failed with the BXM parts, and they want their pound of flesh." She shook her head, her ample bosom wobbling with the movement. "Kadie, you don't want to be around here right now. If they find you, they will get you, and that'll be it. You know how they work."

Each word Della said felt like a nail in her coffin. She had nearly escaped Jonah and his nice, clean lifestyle, where she didn't belong. Now she was being thrust back into a world where she had no experience.

"I'll be fine, Della—" Her words were sharply cut off in mid sentence.

"No. You're coming with me." Jonah pulled her back against him as he reached into his pocket with his other hand, pulling out a card and handing it to Della. "If they come looking for her again, let me know."

Without a word, he hauled Kadie out the door and down to the car. She tried to get away, pulling on the arm that held her, and he looked at her. She grew cold when she saw the chill in his eyes. "If you try to get out, I'll restrain you and fasten you to the fucking seat. Now get in and stay there."

She was witnessing a side she never would have expected of him, and this aspect she understood better than the well-bred, urbane persona she had seen up until now. Kadie sat down, allowing him to climb in and punch the engine.

Jonah whipped the vehicle through the alleys to the building where impounded vessels were kept. He flashed his ID disk and waited until the guard waved them through.

Jonah parked the air-car at the office and his terse, "Stay here," stopped her from following him into the building. He emerged quickly with a number and a grim set to his face. "Follow me."

Okay, so he was pissed. She was too. No one treated her like some pet to be picked up, enjoyed, and then put back on the floor. But she felt no comfort in the small, private rebellion.

* * *

Yep, he'd pissed her off. Too bad. He wasn't in any mood to put up with any more of her half-truths. What the madam had told him made him furious. The rage he contained, barely.

Kadie followed him to the spot where her ship sat, lonely, in the middle of the impoundment yard, and he stopped at the door, waiting for her to enter the ship unlock command. The door swung open and they entered the drab, dark interior.

"Grab some clothing. You can wash them at home." His words were short, but he made no apologies as he followed her down the corridor, their feet echoing in the silence as they entered a spartan room.

No bright colors on the walls, no knickknacks, and no pictures. The ship felt impersonal to him. He didn't know what he'd expected, but it certainly wasn't the gray room and old furnishings that had obviously seen better days. The space was scuffed and marked, though impeccably clean. A bed and a small cupboard she ignored were all that existed in the room and he waited as Kadie opened a small hamper.

He noted it was only half-full and frowned. She said she had no clean clothes. He opened the tiny cupboard, amazed to see that it was empty. She pulled an empty sack from under the bed, clean but threadbare, with a single sheet, no blankets, and an old pillow.

Jonah watched quietly as she pulled a couple of coveralls from the hamper and some old panties and a bra. That's it? That's all her clothes? His stomach hurt as he realized that when she'd said *Oriana's Evadare* was all she had she had meant exactly that. No wonder she thought I had a lot of clothes, he thought ruefully.

"Ready?" he said gruffly as he worked to cover his discomfort with the real evidence of the sparseness of her life.

She nodded wordlessly, avoiding his gaze. Two spots of colors sat on her cheeks, and he could tell she was embarrassed that he had seen the truth. Kadie left the room and headed back toward the door.

"Do you need anything else?"

She shook her head wordlessly, hoisting the small, blue bag over her shoulder, and walked down the bouncing ramp, waiting at the base for him to follow before she entered the code to lock the ship once more.

He led the way to the air-car, the silence growing between them. For the first time in his life, the extent of the luxury he had lived in was brought home sharply, and he felt uncomfortable with the knowledge that he had so much when others had very little.

Jonah watched as she headed to his vehicle and climbed in gripping her small sack of clothing. He started the air-car and made to head home as the portable communications unit lit up.

"Fielding."

"Captain, we have a problem. Kadie Frost has been tagged. We think they may have seen her with you. Word on the street is they want the girl. She *is* still with you, isn't she?"

He glanced at Kadie, the arrested look on her face worrying as she turned back to him. Kadie opened her mouth and shut it again as if she thought better of any possible outburst.

Jonah's chest burned at the thought that they might succeed, snuffing out her vibrant personality. He promised himself it wouldn't happen. There was no way he would allow them to reach her. But if she left him now, there was no way he could guarantee her safety. That was something he wouldn't allow to happen. But he refused to question why, beyond the obvious.

"Yeah. She's here with me right now." His gut churned. They were looking for her. That meant they needed to sort it out quickly. "We are on our way in."

"Negative, Captain. I believe there is still someone in here. Might be best if I came to you." He could hear the concern in his second's voice. "I'll be there in ten." The communications system clicked off as he thumped the console in front of him.

"Fuck! Let's get out of here." Jonah engaged the engine and they were off, whizzing through the air. He knew they had to get back to his place and as quickly as possible. It was secure and safe, of that he had no doubt. Yet another good reason for the choice of his apartment.

They reached his parking bay in seven minutes flat, and he quickly hustled her to the elevator, snatching glances around to ensure no one was watching. The doors opened and they plunged inside, Jonah taking the front and acting as a shield to protect her. She was still clutching her small bag to her chest as the door slid shut. He entered the pass-code and the elevator rose swiftly.

* * *

Kadie watched the play of emotions on Jonah's face.

No one had ever been so thoroughly concerned about her well being and safety before. There was something comforting about it. Right now she had to concentrate on how she could get out of this mess, though.

After all, wasn't that what this whole thing was about? They reached the floor of his apartment and he ushered her in. She watched him stalk around, clearly frustrated and frazzled, running his hands through his beautifully, long hair that had come loose from its bindings during the drive back to the apartment.

"Pop your things in the bedroom. We can do some laundry later, but for now my second and my admin assistant, should be here in a few minutes." The dong of a bell surprised her, but he stalked over to the elevator and pressed a button.

She wandered into the bedroom, dropping the sack to the floor. She didn't want to make a mess of the bed, putting her old, grimy items on it. She slumped. How had it come to this? She had done what she was told, but still managed to make a mess of everything. Kadie mentally shrugged her shoulders. Maybe Jonah would help her sort this out. There really wasn't much else she could do at the moment.

She could hear a woman's voice, and headed into the other room. The most beautiful woman she could imagine stood there in uniform grays. The skirt, short and tight, highlighted a perfectly pert butt; her breasts were the size of grapefruits, again firm and bouncy; and the hair was blonde, short, and curly around a classic, flawlessly pale complexion, deep blue eyes, and bee-stung, red lips teamed with long, thick lashes. *Double fuck!* She was tall and perfectly proportioned. Beside her, Kadie felt short and dirty, little more than a street kid trying to play adult dress up.

Jonah was smiling at the woman, and Kadie wanted to rip her eyes out of her head, the hot flash of jealousy boiling in her throat. She watched the woman checking him out, up and down, like a piece of fine food. The woman was ogling him! Kadie wouldn't be surprised if she reached over and licked him like a candy! The way her eyes lit up and ran over his superb body made Kadie angry.

"Devan brought me along. He has all the information you need," the woman said with a perfectly modulated and educated voice. Kadie seethed. The woman waved an impeccably manicured hand toward the small, squat man standing beside her. His round belly jiggled as he moved forward, leaving little creaking sounds as his shoes moved.

"Kadie, this is Vanessa and Devan. Both are officers in my personal unit. Vanessa is my admin assistant and Devan my personal investigator and second. Guys, meet Kadie Frost."

Vanessa's eyes stopped on her, cold and arctic, as she inclined her regal head toward Kadie.

Bitch!

"Hi, how do you do?" Devan held out a hand, sloppy and wet, as he pumped hers up and down the usual three jerks before letting go. He smiled though and it seemed genuine, with a twinkle in his hazel eyes.

Jonah led them to the table where coffee cups from earlier still sat. He invited them to sit before disappearing into the kitchen. Vanessa followed him into the kitchen and Kadie would have given anything to be there too. But she had her pride. She sure wasn't going to go in there, though she did let her ears strain to see if there was something to hear.

The clanking and clattering in the kitchen told her he was preparing coffees, and she didn't have to wait long to see him carrying a tray with coffee, cream, and sugar to the table. Vanessa held another set of cups. Acting just like the hostess, Kadie thought viciously. This would be a woman to watch. The thought caught her unawares and she tamped it down. After all, Jonah could do what he liked with whom he liked, she reminded herself. He wasn't hers and never would be.

Jonah grabbed Kadie a coffee and pushed it into her hands, black and sugarless, just as she liked it, and she muttered her thanks. He smiled and for an instant his eyes held hers and she shivered.

Vanessa cleared her throat and the two guests grabbed a coffee as Jonah settled into the chair beside Kadie.

"Okay, so what do you know?" He leaned back, fingers steepled, ready to listen.

Chapter Four

Jonah watched Kadie's eyes; they sparked with anger when Vanessa flipped her off. It annoyed him for a second, but he grinned, noting the mutinous expression on her face. He'd seen the brief spurt of anger when he moved to the kitchen and Vanessa followed; he saw the disbelief in her eyes before she hastily hid her emotions.

He needed to do something about Vanessa. It was a problem that Vanessa imagined some relationship between them.

Once he settled at the table, coffee in hand, Devan began outlining what he had heard on the street. "Cap'n, I was down on Millers Lane last night, when one of my informants asked if I'd heard about Kadie Frost. He knew we had her in custody, of course. You know how quickly that info spreads." Jonah gave a silent nod, understanding exactly what Devan was saying. "Well, he said the Consortium were looking for her. She had something they wanted back. I'm guessing the ship or even the BXM parts." He shrugged.

Jonah felt a stab of anger and frustration, but tamped it down.

"Anyway, the informant says they have tagged her. Fifty thousand credits dead and three hundred and fifty thousand alive."

Jonah sat up. That was a hell of a lot of credits. They wanted her alive with that large an amount, so she had some information about who they were. He turned back to her. Kadie's head was bowed and he felt another surge of anger at the unknown, faceless Consortium who wanted her.

Devan continued, "We think whoever was her contact at the Silver Squirrel is actually the person we need to find. However, because we got the goods before she could make delivery, we can't prove anything, except that they were there at the time." He shrugged again, wiping his face with an over-sized handkerchief.

"Then we need a plan, a sting, to catch these bastards in the act." Jonah grabbed his coffee mug. The heat of the coffee that sloshed over the rim scalded him. He ignored the pain as he thought about the information Devan had just shared.

Devan nodded and Vanessa reached out for his hand. He snatched it away before she could make contact. The thought of her cold skin touching him made his skin crawl. The only woman he wanted to touch him was Kadie.

Kadie's small, slight frame made him feel strong and manly, and the thought heated his blood more. He thanked the stars he was wearing loose pants, because once again he was aroused, his erection standing at attention.

Kadie looked at him and he smiled. *I'm gone on her already. I just need to make sure she's gone on me as well.* The thought should have terrified him, but instead he felt a warm glow suffusing him. He needed time.

Vanessa opened her mouth and he flicked his eyes toward her, reading her as she caught sight of the secret smile between him and Kadie. Vanessa's lips tightened and flattened. She may be perfect, but to his mind she was a shade too perfect. He needed a woman who was exciting, inventive, and didn't overthink how she presented herself while making love. That was what he could expect with Vanessa and the thought left his stomach churning again.

Devan interrupted. "Jonah, there's no budget at the moment for any form of witness protection. Those funds have been used up with cleaning out the ranks."

Jonah nodded, accepting Devan's words for what they were. Resources in the unit were tight. "Are there funds anywhere else?" Jonah looked to Vanessa and she preened.

"Jonah, I don't think there is a spare credit left to pay for anything."

He closed his eyes, spinning ideas in his head. There might be a way yet. With difficulty, he dragged his thoughts back to the matter before them. An idea formed quickly and he smiled, sure it would work, if he could get Kadie to agree.

"Here's what we're going to do. Put it out that Kadie hooked up with me, thinking she would be able to get the BXM parts back from us. We'll go through the motions of releasing the parts to her. We need it to seem furtive and underhand though. As if we're breaking the rules for her. She will make out like she can't get the items to the buyer, but wants to return them to the supplier. We grab them and then follow through."

Vanessa's eyes bulged. "But, Jonah, that will only catch one of them, not the lot. Why jeopardize everything you have worked for to close such a small and unimportant case?" Her voice squeaked at the end with a slight nasal quality that made him clench his teeth.

"No. It just gives us a tangible link to the Consortium. They will either expect us to arrest the buyer or want everything back when Kadie arrives at the Silver Squirrel. Either way, we have a workable situation." He nodded. This plan would work. He was sure of it. He hadn't yet told anyone the final part of the plan. He could keep her safe then, and close by. At least long enough to get her to explore what future they might have between them.

Devan stood up. "Cap'n, can you give me a day to achieve this? We need to ensure it's believable, and I want to be sure we trap the mole in the unit at the same time. Plus, if we take our time, it will seem far more believable."

Jonah assessed Devan. A good, hardworking, and honest investigator had been his initial impression of the man. The more he knew him, the more respect he had for his skills as well as the man who hid beneath the veneer of laziness.

"I also think you need a formal agreement for this to work best. You know, like a marriage. We can get it nullified in twelve hours with the right paperwork in place, surmising we can prove the act took place for the purposes of the investigation."

Devan's words dropped through the air, and Jonah sucked in a breath before adding, "Yes, I think that would be wise. It also saves the department from spending money on protecting our witness, and others won't question why we are always together."

It's the perfect way to keep her close and it might give me enough leverage to maybe start to make it a lifetime commitment. Jonah smiled. Perfect.

* * *

Kadie's stomach dropped. Marriage? Only the rich did that, didn't they? Her head whirled as Vanessa and Devan stood to leave.

The woman radiated what could only be described as hate in great big, oily waves. *Damn.* The woman may be a bitch, and a first class one at that, but she worked with Jonah, so Kadie would accept it. For now. But privately, Kadie did wonder if she wasn't just setting herself up for a fall, taking on the woman who seemed to think she had a hold on Jonah. And then there were those pesky feelings that rose at inappropriate times...the ones she really didn't want to label jealousy and longing.

Jonah winked at her. She really needed to get her body into the same thought pattern as her brain. Nothing could come of the association, she told herself firmly, but that didn't stop her traitorous heart from whispering things she could only wish for. Love? Marriage? Why not? Now you are mixing with his type, perhaps you too could have permanency and love?

"We'd better get you outfitted then and organize a ceremony as quickly as possible. We need to share our love at first sight story with the world, and make sure everyone believes it."

She gulped at his words. "Come on, let's check the screen and see what we can find for you to wear." He smiled at her, and she saw Vanessa's face, a mixture of hate, envy, and something else boiling in her eyes.

Jonah grabbed her by the hand as the elevator doors shut, leaving them alone again and flicked onto the shopping page, before he started scanning lists of dresses, gowns, and clothing.

"You don't need the trappings you know." The words sounded strangled even to her ears. How could she do this? Take the things he was giving, when she felt like such a fraud. A fraud in love, whispered that voice in her brain again. She stopped in her tracks. Love? Had she honestly fallen for him? The answer hit her in the face. She sure had. *Damn! Fuck! Shit!*

He looked at her, and for an instant, she wanted to leap into his arms, screaming about her emotional state, but years of self-imposed training to stay invisible kept her quiet. "You need to give the impression we're building a lifetime commitment here. Now then, what size are you?"

She nearly yelped, controlling herself again. How would she know? She wore coveralls for heaven's sake! Even her underwear was one size fits most. She sighed, tamping down the feeling of frustration that rose in her chest.

"I don't know."

He quirked an eyebrow at her. "You don't know?" He repeated her answer and she shrugged.

"I wear coveralls. My underwear is one size fits all. I get them when I need some. I don't need any more right now."

He smiled at her and she caught her breath. Damn, he was so sexy. "Right then. Let's go shopping and you can be fitted."

That surprised her. Didn't men hate shopping? "There's no need. I don't need anything else." She wailed the words, but he just smiled enigmatically at her, grabbing her hand and towing her to the elevator.

"Building a life, remember?"

She was so fucked!

* * *

Jonah dragged her around the shopping mall. Kadie was stiff and unresponsive at the start, but he reminded her regularly that the Authority Department would foot the bills from the proceeds of crime fines and slowly she began to settle.

He pushed her into a boutique as soon as they arrived, thinking to outfit her immediately. The woman in there fussed over Kadie after she got past the old coverall she was wearing, of course. She'd started sighing over her petite sizing and thick red hair.

"Most people can only achieve that color with chemicals. Is it natural?"

Kadie just stared at the woman as if she were mad, and he answered. "Absolutely." At his answer, the clerk beamed.

Within the hour, Kadie had shoes, bags, and even a couple of hats. She wore a pantsuit in green that made her red hair into a glowing halo. A small, gold chain graced her neck and she wore boots of soft leather with a tiny heel. She looked like she belonged with him and he hoped it would settle some of her nerves.

Jonah grinned at her. Now as they walked along, every man turned to look at her and he knew she was in a state of total bewilderment.

He steered her toward an intimates shop. She balked at more than three pairs of underwear, but let the assistant fit her anyway under his urging. While she was in the fitting room, he walked around throwing nightgowns, thongs, and even sheer bras on the desk of the clerk while he'd simply smiled.

The clerk grinned at him, broader with each item he added to the growing pile. He envisaged Kadie wearing them for him and, even better, taking them off.

Jonah started to sweat at the thought, but was enjoying himself too much to stop. So instead, he continued choosing some more exotic intimate wear as well. "I want all these in her size. Bill me now and send them to this address."

The clerk packed the piles of underwear into packages and had placed them behind the desk out of sight. He barely had time to scribble the address on the slip when Kadie came out. Plain, white panties and bra sets in hand. He smiled secretly at the packages he knew were full of pink, red, black, and even blue underwear he had ordered for her and paid for the items in her hands, winking at the clerk as they left the shop together. All the other items would be waiting when they got home and he hoped he might get her to try some on for his viewing pleasure.

"I don't need anything else."

He dragged her to an eveningwear shop where she stared at the multitudes of gowns in luxurious materials as they entered. He didn't just want a gown for her, though. It had to be the gown. The one that made her feel like a fairy princess.

Jonah gazed around only to spy it in the corner. It was a deep green sheath that would mold to her body, and he knew there was underwear in the packages he had bought that would be perfect underneath.

"Let's try that." He pointed to the gown and the clerk smiled.

"We've had that one for ages. I can even do a deal if it fits."

He nodded and the clerk scurried to grab the gown from the corner where it had been hanging. The clerk dragged Kadie into the fitting room, dress draped over her arm, and when Kadie emerged he felt his heart stop. The gown hugged every curve lovingly, showing her small, creamy breasts rising against the silk, and his breath caught. It was perfect.

She was clearly overcome as she exited the dressing room. Her eyes shone and she couldn't seem to stop checking herself in the mirror.

"We'll take it. Now, do you have matching shoes?" They swiftly paid for the gown and he accepted the large bag, hanging it over his arm and then slipping her arm through his.

"You're spending too much," Kadie wailed.

Jonah smiled. He rarely met a woman who complained he spent too much on them. It was a refreshing change. Then again, that was his Kadie to a T.

"Just a few more things and we're done." He dragged her to another small boutique, purchasing trousers and blouses. He figured she wasn't a dress girl usually, though one small, polka-dot dress called to him, and he could imagine it gracing her curves. She argued hard that she didn't need a dress, but once it was on, he watched her smooth it down over her delicious curves. They bought it and shoes to match, together with a bag. In fact, they matched every outfit with shoes and accessories. He had the money and no qualms at using it.

The last stop was a jeweler.

They would need bands for the ceremony, and she would have argued, but he stopped it by pressing his mouth against hers. The jeweler thought they were in love, bringing an array of golden and silver bands. He sent them back, telling the jeweler he wanted nothing so ordinary, and finally settled on a platinum set, inlayed with a dazzling array of precious stones. All the time, Kadie watched him, looking shocked at the growing mound of purchases waiting beside them.

Chapter Five

Kadie stepped into the bedroom before stopping still. The sight of parcels and packets mounded everywhere startled her. A series of bags with the lingerie shop imprinted sat on top of boxes and she walked over, picking them up and peering inside. Tissue paper wrapped items lay inside, a rainbow of colors and items. There had to be at least fifteen bags from the lingerie shop alone. Her stomach clenched at the sight, but a frisson of excitement wound through her veins. Never had she seen so many clothes meant for her. Then reality set in.

What on Centauri had he done?

She stumbled back to the bed, slumping down and putting a hand over her eyes. How could she possibly make restitution on all this? Her head spun at the idea of the credits he'd spent on her.

"Kadie? You need to shower and dress. Get ready for the ceremony." Jonah's voice echoed through the apartment, and she closed her eyes. God, how she wished it was for real.

She stripped off the beautiful outfit he bought her first and headed for the shower. Hot water ran from the nozzle and she stood still, feeling the unfamiliar warmth running over her nude body. She quickly completed her ablutions, stepping back out of the shower stall, grabbing the fluffy towel, and drying quickly as she moved to the bedroom. One pair of underwear lay on the bed, but she spied bags with the lingerie boutique symbol sitting against the wall. Kadie's curiosity got the better of her as she looked at the door quickly. Then, rushing over, she grabbed the bags and emptied them onto the bed. She ripped away the tissue paper and saw the items contained within.

But it was still the set on the bed that seemed right, a strapless bra, the same color as her gown, and matching panties. Whispering a quick, silent apology to the plain white sets she'd chosen, she slipped the set that matched the dress on and started to pull the gown over her head. Feeling it slide over her body, she thought this the softest cloud of silk and said a silent thank you to whoever made the gown for putting the zipper on the side.

The shoes in the next bag were a perfect match for the dress and she slipped them on, exiting the room as she wrestled with her hair. She tamed it and let it coil behind her head. The tap of his footsteps in the other room hurried her along and she snatched open the door to the living area.

He waited for her. His black suit molded to his muscular body, and her mouth dried. He wore an impeccable white shirt and his hair was tied back with a silver hair tube. When he looked at her, he smiled and she wanted to faint at the bubble of emotion that lodged in her chest.

"You are exquisite." His words rumbled from between smiling lips.

"You scrub up pretty good too."

They were heading to the judge's chambers for a private ceremony, and her stomach churned. It was all such a lie and she was the biggest fraud. How could she say the words, knowing she felt as she did?

On the other hand, she couldn't say no either.

The feelings within her jumbled wildly. Misery consumed her on one hand, yet elation warred with the negative feelings on the other.

Jonah slipped her hand through the crook of his arm and they headed toward the elevator. It pinged and swung open and he pulled her inside. "Remember to smile. We are madly in love. The whole love at first sight thing happening. We are pledging our undying love to each other." His words sounded so lighthearted and shame coursed through her system. She was about to tell the biggest lie of her life.

Kadie waited quietly beside him as the elevator stopped. They stepped out together and walked to the vehicle. He flicked the switch and it started, rumbling underneath her, and shot out of the parking spot. He drove fast, the forces pushing her back into the seat as Kadie tried to control her roiling emotions.

When Jonah pulled up outside the old building, he slipped out of the air-car, hurried around to help her out, and took a minute to make sure it locked. Then he pulled her up the long, white steps into the old and imposing building.

The building itself was empty of life as they hurried along the corridors toward the office. The sound of their footsteps echoed in the cavernous rooms, heels tapping on the marble floors, and the cool air caressed her skin. Jonah opened the heavy, dark, wooden doors to reveal a woman sitting at an old wood table.

"Good evening, Captain. Ms. Frost, it's a pleasure to meet you. The judge is expecting you. Please go through." The staffer signaled that they should move through the door behind her, so they kept going, entering the chamber. An older man smiled at their approach and a sense of giddiness filled Kadie.

"Welcome, Jonah. This is your delightful lady? I am so pleased you chose to come to me tonight." He waved toward some seats and ran them through the ceremony and their responsibilities.

Kadie felt like a fraud. Worse than a fraud. The words ran like a refrain through her head as they took their places in front of the judge.

The staffer who had followed them through from the other room and a janitor acted as witnesses to the wedding.

At the end, the ring weighed down her finger like a ball and chain. *I will smile though, just as he told me to do. God knows, I'll smile until my face aches if that's what he needs.*

* * *

Kadie was upset. He could see it in the set of her shoulders, the way her face froze into a smile that he could easily see was fake, and the empty look in her eyes.

He carefully helped her to find the way outside the building and into the vehicle that was waiting for them curbside where it had been left. A huge difference from their trip to The Light House.

"Come on, let's go home and grab something to eat." He would have preferred to take her to a fancy restaurant to celebrate, but tonight was for them alone and he wasn't sure of her reaction to a restaurant, so he had made alternative arrangements back at the building. He was glad he had organized for a meal to be ready, complete with candles and fine wine. It was their wedding night and he intended to enjoy it.

He intended to ensure she enjoyed it too.

Jonah parked and once more they made their way silently up the elevator to the level where he lived. The doors slid open without a sound and they stepped inside. Dinner sat waiting, the silver service he had ordered on the table in the room, the air filled with the perfume of real flowers and the aroma of the meal. Lights winked and glowed from candles on the table.

He turned and took her in his arms. "Welcome home, Mrs. Fielding."

She looked stunned, and he swooped in kissing her on the lips. He deepened the kiss until her arms crept up around his neck and held on. Finally Kadie was kissing back. He could feel the shaking start in her system as the need washed over him.

Jonah raised his head. "Let's eat." He pulled her to the table, picking up the wine from the bucket and pouring two glasses, and then he lifted the dome from her plate and did the same with his.

Making sure this was something she would remember forever, he sat beside her, lifting his glass. "To us. May it be everything we want." He meant the words. He wanted everything with her, but knew she wasn't ready to hear that yet. So he kept the conversation through the meal light.

Dessert was the most delightful confection of fine Pastovov fruits and fresh Carthanian creams in a pastry case. Light and fluffy, yet deliciously exotic; the perfect meal, he felt, to celebrate their marriage. He plied her with the wines. Fine wines to accompany the food. They were both fresh to the taste and chilled perfectly.

At the end of the meal, he stood and beckoned to her, turning on the music console before pulling her into his arms. They twirled and danced around the room and he felt energized by the feel of her body moving against his, making him hot to touch her, kiss her, love her.

The touch of lips ignited the fire within him that had smoldered all day. Jonah pushed closer, feeling her desire rage as she opened her mouth to him. She tasted sweet from the wine and fruits, and he claimed her mouth and tongue with his own.

His hands slipped over her shoulders, bare in the beautiful gown. Her creamy skin shone by candlelight, making her hair glow. Kadie's fingers pushed on his coat, working it over his shoulders, and she opened one button after another on his shirt before tugging at his tie. Once free, the tie went over her shoulder, but he couldn't make himself care about the scrap of material.

Fingers touched under his shirt and he shuddered in reaction. His fingers quested for the fastening of her dress. He found the zipper and pulled it down, inch by inch, before carefully pushing the gown from her body. His mouth traced the fine line of her throat, and he listened to her gasp for breath.

Finally, she stood in only her shoes and underwear in the candlelight. He had never seen such beauty in his life. "You are exquisite." His words were hoarse with the emotions he fought to hold within him.

The bra he had chosen for her, jeweled green that matched her gown, barely covered the luscious skin of her breasts and hid the pert, pink nipples he knew lay beneath the satiny material. It matched the triangle of lace that hid her hot, wet core from his gaze.

She watched him as he slipped out of his pants and underwear, letting his erection spring free into the night air. Kadie wet her lips, which were pink and bee-stung from his kisses. He ached to join his body to hers.

Her violet eyes, smoky in the light, and heavy lids took in the sight of his body and he knew she liked what she saw. Her delicate hands, callused from years of hard work, touched him intimately. Kadie's fingers slid softly over his jutting erection and then traveled down to the springy hairs that lay at its base. She caressed him slowly, feeling the weight of his balls in her hand.

He moved, just a small nudge. But, God help him, he couldn't keep still, and when she knelt on the floor, opening her mouth to pull him inside, he nearly exploded. Her mouth rubbed up and down and her tongue didn't stop.

The glorious suction was nearly his undoing as he groaned and burned beneath her touch. His fingers tangled in her hair.

Unable to wait any longer, Jonah grabbed her, pulling her up his body, thrusting an eager hand down her panties as the other worked at the clasp of her bra. Jonah freed those beautiful, firm breasts from the confines of the lacey material, and then clumsily pushed her panties down her legs, baring her to his view.

"Don't leave me. I need you with me." Her voice filled the air as his brain warred with his triumphant heart. He finally had her naked, panting and wet, just for him. He couldn't wait any longer. He lifted her against his body and thrust into her as she wrapped her legs around his waist.

Kadie hung on for dear life as she undulated against him, her hips moving wildly. The feel of her delicious, warm, and wet core pushed him over the edge. He felt his climax approach, but held on to his fast slipping composure until the first of her ripples began as she started to orgasm in his arms. Then he let go of his control. He pumped her, harder and faster, fingers digging firmly into the flesh at her waist, feeling the explosion as his body released, jetting into her warmth.

His eyes closed, he held her still against him, loving her.

* * *

Kadie woke, Jonah's heavy arm crossed over her body. She ached in places she hadn't realized could ache. Her legs spasmed slightly in response to their athletic lovemaking the night before. Her body, especially between her legs, was tender. Kadie opened her eyes, knowing exactly where she was. In his arms, in his bed, after the most amazing sex of her life. *Again*. Damn!

He grunted in his sleep and she turned slightly to view him. In sleep, Jonah was just as sexy as awake. She noticed his broad, muscular chest, free of hairs, and his tapered waist so perfect. That awesome erection of his. Hang on. Erection?

Kadie let her eyes flick up to his and saw him watching her. Jonah grinned and she did too in response. She could feel the smile steal over her face.

He swooped in for a hard kiss. "No time now. We need to dress and get ready, but tonight, you're all mine. And I plan to eat you all up." He grinned and God help her, she grinned back. He rose from the bed, naked and so ready that she had to look away, otherwise she would beg for another round of mind-blowing sex. As Jonah had said, they just didn't have time.

Except on my side it wasn't just sex. Not anymore. The thought sobered her. She rose. *If I hang around, I'll embarrass him with some ill thought out comment about forever, hearts, and roses. Love.*

She hurried to her bedroom, pulled on some clothes, and joined him in the lounge, surprised he was ready for her, cup of coffee in hand. She took it from him, gratefully sipping the bitter brew. "Thanks."

"My pleasure."

She drained the cup, and as she took it to the kitchen to rinse it, he walked in. "I suppose it's time to go."

Kadie watched him dread growing in the pit of her belly. "Yeah, I guess. Look, I promise to follow every instruction, but please...stay safe. Okay? I know these areas well. They are rough."

She swallowed the lump that threatened to choke her. She

could never forgive herself if anything happened to him because of her actions.

He reached out a hand, a soft hand, touching the side of her face, and the desire to nuzzle it nearly overwhelmed her. "You may have grown up in the slums, Kadie, but you don't live there anymore. You stay safe too."

He obviously wanted to say something more, his hand holding her still for just a little longer and she waited. He must have thought better though, shaking his head as a small smile appeared on his lips.

They left the apartment, heading to the Silver Squirrel. He pulled up, a worried expression on his face. "It'll be fine." She started to get out of the car and he stopped her.

"Take this tracker." He slipped it into her hand and she lodged it in her boot. As she lifted her head, he grabbed her, pulling her into a quick, tight kiss.

At the back of the vehicle, she hoisted out the box of parts they had collected from Devan in the parking area of the apartment building.

"Remember, you're returning them. Nothing more."

She nodded shakily and stepped away from the air-car. She knew he wanted to come in, but they had agreed it wasn't wise. Kadie moved to the door, checking the box one last time. All she needed to do was hand the box back to the person she had collected it from. Nothing more. It should be simple, she told herself, but she didn't feel too sure.

The door swung open and she stepped inside another world, seedy and dark. The smell of bodies, washed and unwashed, hit her, just like other smells, most of them unsavory. Kadie gasped as the scents hit her system.

Her stomach churned, and the box in her arms started to feel like it weighed a ton. as she gulped down the bubble of hot bile that rose in her throat.

Devan and Jonah had installed micro trackers on each of

the parts, so all she had to do was hand them over. It would be easier said than done though, she thought. Nervous and shaky, she stepped through the doorway and into the room they had hopefully called The Lounge.

Grimy, red seating, which appeared stained in daylight waited in the room beyond. Maybe once, years ago, it had been plush, but now it appeared more like the leavings of a thousand bar fights and smelled worse.

Kadie picked her way over a body lying supine on the floor. The stench wafted in the air as the beat of the music vibrated throughout the room. Too much to drink or perhaps mixing it with Dream Chaser, a nasty drug that produced stupor on the tail of its high, but she had no time to check. She glanced around, seeking the man in the half-light.

The raucous noise seemed to stop as Kadie looked around. People stood, making their way out of the room. Devan had hunched into the back corner, crouched over a drink. She would bet he hadn't sipped it. She certainly wouldn't. You never knew what you might pick up in the Silver Squirrel. And that wasn't limited to partners, male or female.

By the bar, the man stood in his gray jacket with his back to her. She privately thought the coat would be as grimy in the subdued lighting as it would be in the daylight. She moved forward and carefully sat down on the stool next to him, placing her hand on his shoulder briefly, and then dropping it away. The material at his shoulder was slimy and vaguely grainy. She hesitated at the thought that the residue could be the leavings of a dozen sexual encounters.

"I got the BXM parts back." She breathed the words as she signaled for the drink she wouldn't touch.

"I don't want the parts. My buyer does." The words were cold and she felt sick at the hard tone in his voice. The drink sloshed onto the sticky bar in front of her. She threw a credit disk down, nodding as it disappeared into the hand reaching out.

"I'm being watched. I need to get them back to you, so you can find another courier and I can get my ship cleared."

"You married the captain. You can do anything now." The words stopped her dead. The words she had dreaded hearing rang through her mind.

"Nope. I can't. I won't risk his name to do this. I'm returning the parts." She shoved them toward him, when she felt someone at her back.

"You will deliver them. Then you will deliver others too," a woman's voice whispered into her ear.

"What if I refuse?" Her voice shook, no matter how much he had prepared her for this in the vehicle. Dear God, she wasn't cut out for subterfuge and she wished for a way out.

"Then you will regret it. Your man will be tagged first though." The words whispered quietly in her ear and she made to turn around, but the anonymous woman grabbed her hair, keeping her head still. She got a glimpse of black hair, long arms, and the reflection of metal on a wrist. She knew that bracelet.

Shit!

Someone in the Authority Department knew what she was doing, she was sure, and the thought scared her. Even worse though, Kadie knew the woman behind her. The thoughts came quickly. She knew the woman; because she had run the juvie hostel Kadie had lived in. Kadie knew she had connections.

"I will give *Oriana's Evadare* to you, just don't tag him. Okay?" She knew it wouldn't be enough, but she needed leverage. A distraction so she could get out of the Silver Squirrel. "You can have that. Just let me go and don't tag him." There would be others in the gang. She had been aware that this couldn't be a single person sting, but she would never have expected this.

"No. You haven't outlived your usefulness yet. Now, I expect you to deliver the BXM parts, as agreed. Then come back here. They will give you an item that I need. We can talk then." The man rose and she made one last ditch try.

"I don't want to do this. Just let me walk away."

He laughed. It wasn't a happy laugh though; it just sent cold shivers down her spine. "Ask me again, and I will tag him immediately. Just for fun. Now be a good, little girl and do as you're told." He flicked his hands, dismissing her. She took the opportunity, scooping up the hated box and moving as quickly as she could out of the lounge. She didn't look back.

At the door of the Silver Squirrel she could feel someone watching. Without a backward glance, she grabbed the door, hauled it open, and hurried down the steps.

Chapter Six

Jonah watched as Kadie hurried down the steps. What the hell was she still doing with the parts? The idea of the sting was to set them up, not bring them back! He hadn't liked the thought of her going in there alone. Sure, he had Devan in there backing her up, but damn, he hated the fact she was unprotected. He scraped his fingers through his hair in frustration.

Kadie hurried over to the vehicle, looking white and upset, tear tracks on her face. He wanted to grab her in his arms, but he forced himself to stay, patiently waiting in the air-car. Not something he did well, he admitted.

The minute she was in the vehicle though, all bets were off. "What went wrong?"

"They wouldn't let me hand them over. They...they threatened to..." Her words died away and the anger he held in check rose in his chest once more.

"They threatened what?" *If they so much as touched one hair on her head, I will crucify them in the courts, after I've finished tearing them to pieces physically. Slowly.*

His hands fisted as the tide of rage began to consume him, licking at his insides like a burning flame.

"They threatened to tag you. I couldn't let them. I've got you mixed up in the whole mess and I should never have allowed that. I mean you're a good and honest man." She choked the words out, tears tracking down her pale face and she swallowed. "I've caused you more trouble than I'm worth. I'm so sorry." She was sobbing quietly, the words came out a mixed jumble from her lips and he wanted to grab her. Reassure her. Hold her.

"And then you had to marry me. I don't want you to think badly of me, and I know it's just a sham marriage but still, I want you to know I have always tried to do the right thing." The words escaped in a wet wail, ending with an inelegant sniff.

He pulled her further into the vehicle then shot off after checking she had buckled up. The sooner they got away from there the better. She continued to sniff in the seat next to him and he grabbed her hand.

"Okay, so did you find out anything more about the Consortium?" His words were harsh. *Damn*! He couldn't help that. He worried about her, but his job meant doing the hard things nobody else would. Difficult enough with his concern for her safety, he allowed privately.

Jonah handed her a handkerchief and she blew her nose and wiped her face. He winced as he watched her actions.

"Yeah. I did. I actually got a micro transmitter on the man. When I grabbed his attention, I put it on the shoulder of his jacket. He had a woman working with him from the juvie hostel. I would think you will find that most of the marks have come from there." Her words were still watery, but at least a little more settled.

He checked the rearview mirror at the space behind them. A black vehicle followed closely.

"We have a tail." He had expected something along those lines, though. His fingers touched the small gray button on the console and a face flashed onto the small screen.

"What's up, Jonah?"

"Remember I said you owed me? Well, I need to collect now. I have a tail and we have a micro-tracker fitted to the supplier of the BXM parts."

Kadie was peering through the rear of the vehicle. There was horror on her face. "Oh, Jonah! What are we going to do? I thought this sort of thing only happened in vids!" She turned around to him and the tears were back, together with a huge dollop of fright, if he didn't miss the signs. "I really messed up this time. I should never have put you in this position! I mean, why would I do that to the man I love?"

He heard the words, saw the minute she realized what she said, her hand slapping over her mouth as she pulled back away from him.

Damn, the woman had seriously bad timing! Even so, the words settled in his chest, filling it and warming him through. "Well, that's a good thing, because I love you too." He grinned at her and then turned back to the communications screen .

"Anyway, Seth, I need you to find the man that Kadie put the tracker on, and get me a unit to pick this vehicle off me. How soon can you arrange that?" The man on the screen grinned at him. He had obviously heard the whole exchange. *Well, damn! So what if they knew?*

"I can have a unit on you, about...now." The wail of sirens split the air as Authority vehicles jammed on either side of the black unit following them.

Jonah grinned, braking and stopping. He turned to Kadie. "Stay here."

He noticed with dismay though, that she followed his actions rather than orders, getting out of the air-car as he did.

He sighed and surged toward the car. He would have to teach her to follow his directions, when it came to safety. Now wasn't the time to focus on that though.

Jonah reached for the handle of the black vehicle, pulling it open. Inside were two men, burly and muscular, young and likely dangerous. His anger rose, stronger than usual. Adrenaline pumped, working through his system. Jonah stepped in front of Kadie as his men swarmed. They pulled the men out and restrained them.

"Get them into interrogation and see what you can find out." He turned and Kadie was watching him, her mouth open. He couldn't help himself, he grabbed her to him and swooped in to kiss her luscious lips. The cherry of the lip gloss she wore made her taste more delicious as he pulled her body snug against his.

Damn! He was getting hard. Again. This was going to be interesting, if he kept getting aroused every time she was near. Jonah grinned at the thought.

* * *

She felt his body hard against hers. Every time he touched her she went up in flames.

And boy did she want to fan them. Jonah pulled away and she mewled her dissatisfaction. Then realized she was standing on a street, in daylight, just about ready to strip the Captain of Authority down to nothing and climb on top of him. She sighed. This could be a very big problem if she wanted to horizontal hustle with him whenever he was near. She grinned and started back toward his unit.

Remembering what he said in the car stopped her dead in her tracks. *He said he loved me.* "Did you mean what you said in the vehicle?"

He nearly barreled into her, stopping as she blurted out

the words. "When I said what?" he teased her. She could see it in the glow in his eyes. "The one about the tail? Yeah." He watched her, his eyes settled on hers, as if daring her to ask the question.

She took a deep breath and plunged, her words leaving her no way to recall them. *Time to take a chance, Kadie.* "About loving me?" She held her breath, not blinking as her heart rate sped up in her chest.

"Oh, that."

Her shoulders slumped, and her heart shrivelled in her chest. She felt sick and sad and sorry for herself at his response.

He moved closer and she made to move away, but he crowded in, gathering her in his arms. She went stiff against his insidious warmth, his mouth so close to her ear. "Yeah I meant it. I want everything with you."

She was sure he was going to kiss her, but he pulled back, staring deeply into her eyes, making her nearly faint with the intensity that burned her from the inside out. A beeping sound called insistently from the vehicle. Jonah swore inventively.

Kadie smiled. That was the sort of thing she would do, not her Jonah. But there wasn't time to dwell on the thought as he pulled her to the vehicle and pressed the button for the communications center.

"What?" The word was terse.

The face she had seen earlier swam in front of her passion muddled eyes. "We got them. I have a team in position now. They are about to emerge from the Silver Squirrel. I thought you might like to be there."

She knew her eyes had widened with shock and Seth, on the other end, waited for Jonah's response.

"Yeah, I'm on my way. I'm bringing Kadie with me." He grunted and hit the accelerator. He pulled the air-car upward this time though. He didn't engage his sirens, but poured on a burst of speed. He turned off the communications unit.

She gripped the side of her seat as he flew recklessly, in her mind, back toward the Silver Squirrel.

"We get to finish this later. At home."

She shivered at his words, and tiny explosions of pleasure erupted throughout her body. She was hot, ready, and horny. *Shit!*

The unit hurried through the night, and they saw the Silver Squirrel ahead, the ugly, squat building that sat in the middle of the slum district. He pulled into a grungy alley a block away. They still had a good view and she could see vehicles dotted all around.

Devan moved forward with Vanessa in tow. She scowled blackly at Kadie, picking her way through the grotty refuse that littered the ground. Vanessa had obviously heard about their exchange on the communications board, because she barely glanced at Jonah, giving him the cold shoulder.

Devan turned to the two of them as they waited quietly. "We have the vehicles ready to go, and thanks to Kadie's efforts, we should be able to pull these two in. I recognize the woman though. She's Sandy Blakeny. She ran the juvie hostel near the port. It was the roughest in town from what I remember." He looked at Kadie sadly. "Turns out, she had a file so large they needed containers for her arrest sheets alone. Never knew how she achieved her position at the hostel, unless it was an in-kind sort of payment." Devan sighed heavily and glanced toward the building. "Anyway, Kadie was spot on when she thought the marks came from there. Every last one. I also think I found our mole, another juvie inmate, so we'll be following that up too. While Ms. Blakeny is considered the Ms. Big here, I'm fairly sure we should be able to crack the case with the information we now have. Good work, Kadie." Devan reached over, his sloppy, wet handshake heartfelt.

"Thanks, Devan. Vanessa..." She had been about to reach out, but Vanessa turned and walked away. Kadie sighed again.

"Don't worry about Vanessa, she found out about you two over the communications unit and thought she honestly had a chance with the captain beforehand. She has an issue with competition. Captain, you may wish to consider a transfer for her to another section, for your own peace of mind."

Jonah stood quietly by during the conversation, shaking his head.

Kadie could see he was lost with the machinations of women, and she grabbed his hands. "I'll explain it all later." She winked at him and he smiled that slow, sexy smile that melted her bones.

* * *

She winked at him, and his body was still heating up. All he could do was smile back at her before turning to Devan. "Are all the teams in place?"

Devan was more than capable in everything he did. Jonah had already considered Devan for the position of Assistant Captain of Authority, which would become available soon. It was right that Devan should be rewarded for his loyalty and abilities.

During the regime of corruption, he had been sidelined and ignored, but thankfully times had changed here on Centauri. This action was yet another nail in the coffin of the corrupt past.

"Yes, Captain, they've just confirmed their locations." Devan put a finger to his ear, a transmission was obviously coming in and Jonah noted the concentration on the other man's face. "They're moving now."

The three walked to the end of the alley, staying within the shadows as they watched two people strut out of the building. They moved into the street and a black car slid alongside to pick them up. Just as they reached for the door, Jonah and Devan's men swarmed over the couple, pushing them to the ground.

"Clear." Devan spoke quietly.

Jonah nodded. It was time to move in now. He grabbed Kadie's hand and they walked together, forward toward Jonah's men who were already pulling the driver and her friend from the vehicle. He could tell the instant their mark recognized the woman at his side. She stiffened slightly and looked at him.

"Do you know the driver?"

She nodded. "Yeah, that's Caryn. We bunked together in the juvie home."

He nodded, that made sense. Grow your own thugs had never gone out of fashion. Jonah waited as his men restrained the four. Vehicles were brought around and they bundled the prisoners into the wagons, the restraints used efficiently to hold them in place.

The woman, Caryn, looked at Kadie, anger and hate lighting her eyes. Kadie stood quietly, watching and rising above the insults Caryn yelled at her, though from time to time she flinched at the angry words.

Jonah knew she found it hard, and he was proud of her. His men came over, a team finally, after months of hard work, excising the corruption from within. Each man and woman smiled at the positive outcome of their first major bust. He smiled too. Cracking the BXM gang was something they could all celebrate, and he congratulated his people.

He guided Kadie back to the air-car. She insisted on attending the interrogation, and he understood that she needed to see and hear everything. He knew it represented a symbolic cutting of the cord that bound her to the past, the one that stopped her from moving on to a new life.

The one he planned to share with her.

* * *

They entered the apartment. The night was about to give way to morning, as the three suns of Centauri peeked over the horizon. He steadied her as if he knew she was exhausted. What a week.

First, collapsing on the floor in front of Jonah hadn't been in any plan. Finding a scorching hot man who was nurturing and caring had shocked her system.

Lastly, falling in love, getting arrested, becoming a witness and then main player in the BXM sting took it out of a girl.

Kadie looked back. Jonah. Her husband. She tingled at the meaning behind the words. It wasn't everyday a girl from the slums made good with a man she not only admired and respected, but also loved. Actually, she lusted too, just a little. She giggled a little at the last thought.

He pulled her into his arms. "Tired, are you? Well, now we're home and you can sleep in. Not that I think we'll do much sleeping. Not for a while anyway." His mouth tipped to hers and she raised herself, ready for the kick of passion that never seemed to fade with him around.

They staggered to the bedroom, locked at hip and lip, his hands unbuttoning her clothing, hers grasping his tight, gorgeous butt. They fell together into the bed and rolled. He looked tired, but elated, and they lay on their backs and she smiled. They lay still for just a few minutes before Kadie turned her head, ready to kiss him. She noticed his eyes were closed. His breathing even... *Fuck! He's fallen asleep?*

She leaned over, dropping a light kiss on his lips before rolling back onto her side, watching silently as his chest rose and fell. Thoughts rolled around in her mind. They had a lot to work on, she knew. Kadie wondered how they would begin to sort out her ship, his job, and their lives. How they would make this relationship work. She watched as he slept and the dim glow of the suns changed as they rose in the sky.

His eyes finally opened, and she felt a bubble of happiness. "Did I fall asleep?" His words were drowsy and sleep hazed.

She smiled. "Yep."

"Damn! I wasted time. Come here, my gorgeous wife." He reached over and she pulled away.

He frowned. "What?"

"We need to talk. About us and all this." She let her hands fly around the room. "How we can make it work."

He smiled. "Yeah, we will. Do you know what, though? I love you, you love me, we can build a lifetime together, and to me that is what matters most of all. We are both strong enough that we can and will find a way." He leaned toward her. "We won the jackpot."

"Yeah, we did, didn't we?" She leaned forward. It would be hard, but they were both on the same track.

They would make it work.

She settled her lips on his.

The End

Also by Imogene Nix

<u>Warriors of the Elector</u>

- Star of Ishtar
- Starline
- Starfire
- Star of the Fleet
- Starburst
- The Star of Eternity

The Star of Ishtar & Starline - Print

Starfire & Star of the Fleet - Print

Starburst & The Star of Eternity - Print

Blood Secrets (Re-releasing 2020)

- The Blood Bride
- The Illuminated Witch
- The Sorcerer's Touch

<u>The Search Duology</u>

- Miss Elspeth's Desire
- Miss Isabelle's Craving

<u>Reunion Trilogy</u>

- War's End
- The Assassin
- Executing Justice

The Reunion Trilogy in Paperback

Sex Love & Aliens

- Tangled Webs
- False Webs
- Covert Webs

21st Testing Protocol

- Cyborg: Redux
- Children Of A Greater Evil
- When Evil Came To Stay (Not Yet Released)
- Finis: The War To End All Wars (Not Yet Released)

Celtic Cupid Trilogy

- Blame The Wine
- A Stranger's Embrace
- Revenge On Cupid

The Celtic Cupid Trilogy in Paperback

Zombieology

- The Reset (2018)
- I Dream of Zombies (2019)
- The Six Million Dollar Zombie (Not Yet Released)

Knights of Pleasure

- Silken Knights (Not Yet Released)

Single Titles

The Chocolate Affair (also in Print)

Falling In Love Again (Previously A Sapphire For Karina)

BioCybe (also in Print)

Hesparia's Tears (also in Print)

Tomorrow's Promise

A Bar In Paris (also in Print)

Inheritance Of The Blood (also in Print)

The Plan

Loving Memories (also in Print)

Hero of Heartbreak Hill (also in Print)

Raspberry Dreams (Not Yet Released)

Non Fiction

Self Publishing: Absolute Beginners Guide (With Suzi Love)

Written as Ciara Cave

25 Curated Ways To Get Rid Of Telemarketers

Book Signings for Absolute Beginners

About the Author

Imogene is published in a range of romance genres including Paranormal, Science Fiction and Contemporary. She is mainly published in the UK and USA due to the nature of her tales.

In 2011, Imogene Nix was born in Bondi, NSW during a Romance Readers Convention. From there, there was no stopping her! Imogene sat down and worked tirelessly for 3 months culminating in the books Starline. This book became the first in a trilogy titled, "Warriors of the Elector."

Imogene has successfully been contracted for twenty-five titles and self published three others, under this pseudonym. She has also completed another three and is, like many of her contemporaries, seeking homes for these books—with at least one likely to be self published once ready.

Imogene is a member of a range of professional organisations, including Romance Writers of Australia, (ARRA) Australian Romance Readers Association, Science Fiction Romance Brigade (SFRB), Dark Siders Down Under (the Australian Paranormal, Erotic Writers of Australia, (ALLi) Alliance of Independent Authors, Queensland Writers Centre and most recently Romance Writers of New Zealand.

She also mentors new writers and love to drink coffee, wine & eat chocolate and is parenting 2 spoiled dogs and a ferocious cat!

To contact Imogene
www.imogenenix.net
imogene@imogenenix.net